U0051691

The Rose
of the World
EX-LIBRIS
©DEE TEN PUBLISHING

葉慈詩選／

塵世玫瑰

The Rose of the World

中・英對照雙語版

威廉・巴特勒・葉慈——著

趙 靜——譯

笛藤出版

前　言

唯美詩化的文字，猶如夜幕蒼穹中的密佈星羅，自悠久的歷史長河之中散發出璀璨迷人的耀目光環，是人類精神世界中無價的瑰寶。千百年來，由各種文字所組成的篇章，經由傳遞淬煉，使其在各種文學彙集而成的花園中不斷綻放出絢幻之花，讓人們沉浸於美好的閱讀時光。

作者們以凝練的語言、鮮明的節奏，反映著世界萬象的生活樣貌，並以各種形式向世人展現他們內心豐富多彩的情感世界。每個民族、地域的文化都有其精妙之處，西洋文學往往直接抒發作者的思想，愛、自由、和平，言盡而意亦盡，毫無造作之感。

18 ～ 19 世紀，西洋文學的發展進入彰顯浪漫主義色彩的時期。所謂浪漫主義，就是用熱情奔放的言辭、絢麗多彩的想像與直白誇張的表現手法，直接抒發出作者對理想世界熱切追求與渴望的情感。《世界經典文學 中英對照》系列，精選了浪漫主義時期一些作者們的代表作，包括泰戈爾的《新月集》、《漂鳥集》；雪萊的《西風頌》；濟慈的《夜鶯頌》；拜倫的《漫步在美的光影》；葉慈的《葦間風》。讓喜文之人盡情地徜徉於優美的文字間，領略作者及作品的無盡風采，享受藝術與美的洗禮。本系列所精選出的作品在世界文學領域中皆為經典名作，因此特別附上英文，方便讀者對照賞析英文詩意之美，並可同時提升英文閱讀與寫作素養。

在這一系列叢書當中，有對自然的禮讚，有對愛與和平的歌頌，有對孩童時代的讚美，也有對人生哲理的警示。作者們在其一生中經歷了數次變革，以文字的形式寫下了無數天真、優美、現實、或悲哀的篇章，以無限的情懷吸引著所有各國藝文人士。文學界的名人郭沫若與冰心便是因受到了泰戈爾這位偉大的印度著名詩人所著詩歌的影響，在一段時期內寫出了很多類似的詩作。在世界文學界諸多名人當中有貴族、政治名人、社會名流、也有普羅大眾，他們來自不同的國家、種族，無論一生平順或是坎坷，但其所創作品無一不是充滿了對世間的熱愛，對未來美好世界的無限嚮往。

編按：由於經過時間變遷、地域上的區別，許多遣辭用句也多所改變，為期望能更貼近現代讀者，特將原譯文經過潤飾，希望讀者能以貼近生活的語詞，欣賞葉慈所欲傳達的詩意哲理。

目　錄

悲哀的牧羊人／

有一個人，把「悲傷」當作朋友，

而他，正想著他高貴的知己「悲傷」 ，

邁著輕盈的步子，走在閃閃發光的沙灘，

海浪拍打著沙灘，沙聲窸窣。

他仰天吶喊，要星星從他們那黯淡的王座

俯身給他慰藉，可星星

依然樂於其中暗自竊笑，並不斷地歡唱，

於是，把悲傷當作朋友的人

高喊道：「昏暗的海洋，請聽聽我最傷感的故事吧！」

波濤依舊卷著浪花，發出雄渾的聲音，

在夢中翻滾，從一個山嶺到另一個山嶺。

他，逃離了大海那壯觀的追襲，

在一個遙遠、優雅的山谷中駐足，

把他所有的故事向晶瑩的露珠傾訴。

The Sad Shepherd

There was a man whom Sorrow named his Friend,

And he, of his high comrade Sorrow dreaming,

Went walking with slow steps along the gleaming

And humming Sands, where windy surges wend:

And he called loudly to the stars to bend

From their pale thrones and comfort him, but they

Among themselves laugh on and sing alway:

And then the man whom Sorrow named his friend

Cried out, Dim sea, hear my most piteous story!

The sea Swept on and cried her old cry still,

Rolling along in dreams from hill to hill.

He fled the persecution of her glory

And, in a far-off, gentle valley stopping,

Cried all his story to the dewdrops glistening.

但露珠壓根沒聽，只是在留神

傾聽自己滴滴答答的聲音。

把悲傷當作朋友的人，再次

來到了海邊，找到一只貝殼，心想：

「我要把我沉重的故事講一講，

直到我自己的聲音迴響著，將憂傷

送入一顆中空的、孕育著珍珠的心；

直到我自己的故事重新為我謳歌；

直到我自己的低語令人感到慰藉，

看啊，我多年來的負擔將會悄然離去。」

於是他靠近珍貝的邊緣，輕快地歌唱，

但那獨住海邊的傷心人，

將他所有的歌湮沒在那朦朧的呻吟之中，

在她發狂的旋轉中，又將他遺忘。

But naught they heard, for they are always listening,

The dewdrops, for the sound of their own dropping.

And then the man whom Sorrow named his friend

Sought once again the shore, and found a shell,

And thought, I will my heavy story tell

Till my own words, re-echoing, shall send

Their sadness through a hollow, pearly heart;

And my own talc again for me shall sing,

And my own whispering words be comforting,

And lo!my ancient burden may depart.

Then he sang softly nigh the pearly rim;

But the sad dweller by the sea-ways lone

Changed all he sang to inarticulate moan

Among her wildering whirls, forgetting him.

披風、小船和鞋子／

「是什麼，你把它設計得如此光彩美麗？」

「是一件憂傷的披風：

在人們的眼中，它是多麼可愛啊；

將是這憂傷的披風，

在所有人的眼中。」

「是什麼，你用這遠航飛翔的篷帆來建造？」

「是一隻承載憂傷的小船：

它疾駛在海洋上噢，黑夜又白天，

憂傷地漂泊向前噢，

黑夜又白天。」

「是什麼，你用這樣潔白的羊毛來編織？」

「是一雙悲傷的鞋子，

那輕輕的步履踩得無聲無息，

在人們憂傷的耳中，

倏然而輕輕。」

The Cloak, the Boat and the Shoes

"What do you make so fair and bright?

"I make the cloak of Sorrow:

O lovely to see in all men's sight

Shall be the cloak of Sorrow,

In all men's sight."

"What do you build with sails for flight?"

"I build a boat for Sorrow:

O swift on the seas all day and night

Saileth the rover Sorrow,

All day and night."

"What do you weave with wool so white?"

"I weave the shoes of Sorrow:

Soundless shall be the footfall light

In all men's ears of Sorrow,

Sudden and light."

被偷走的孩子／

斯利什森林所在的陡峭高地浸入湖水之處，

有一個蓊鬱的小島，

蒼鷺振展羽翼，

驚醒了那沉睡的水鼠；

那兒，我們已藏好了裝滿漿果的魔桶，

和偷來的，鮮紅並閃著光亮的櫻桃。

來吧，人間的孩子！

到荒野和沼澤裡來吧，

和精靈手牽著手，

這個世界哭聲太多，可你不懂。

The Stolen Child

Where dips the rocky highland

Of Sleuth Wood in the lake,

There lies a leafy island

Where flapping herons wake

The drowsy water rats;

There we've hid our faery vats,

Full of berries,

And of reddest stolen cherries.

Come away, O human child!

To the waters and the wild

With a faery, hand in hand,

For the world's more full of weeping than you can understand.

那兒，月光銀波蕩漾，

為幽暗的沙礫披上了光芒。

在那遙遠的玫瑰園中，

我們徜徉在古老的舞曲裡，

徹夜踩著步子，

手臂與眼神交錯旋轉，

直到月亮沉入天邊；

我們就這樣不停地跳著，

追逐著晶瑩的泡沫；

然而這個世界充滿了煩惱，

甚至在睡夢中也充斥著焦慮。

來吧，人間的孩子！

到荒野和沼澤裡來吧，

和精靈手牽著手，

這個世界哭聲太多，可你不懂。

Where the wave of moonlight glosses

The dim grey sands with light,

Far off by furthest Rosses

We foot it all the night,

Weaving olden dances,

Mingling hands and mingling glances

Till the moon has taken flight;

To and fro we leap

And chase the frothy bubbles,

While the world is full of troubles

And is anxious in its sleep.

Come away, O human child!

To the waters and the wild

With a faery, hand in hand,

For the world's more full of weeping than you can understand.

那兒，溪流蜿蜒，

從葛蘭卡的山坡沖下，

潛入水草叢間的縫隙，

連一顆星星也游不進去，

我們尋找熟睡的鱒魚，

在它們耳邊竊竊私語，

使它們的夢境波瀾起伏；

輕輕地把身子傾向前方，

倚在蕨草之上，

讓淚水落入年輕的溪流中。

來吧，人間的孩子！

到荒野和沼澤裡來吧，

和精靈手牽著手，

這個世界哭聲太多，可你不懂。

Where the wandering water gushes

From the hills above Glen-Car,

In pools among the rushes

That scarce could bathe a star,

We seek for slumbering trout

And whispering in their ears

Give them unquiet dreams;

Leaning softly out

From ferns that drop their tears

Over the young streams,

Come away, O human child!

To the waters and the wild

With a faery, hand in hand,

For the world's more full of weeping than you can understand.

和我們一同離去的

那個眼神莊嚴的孩子：

他將不再聽到溫暖的山坡上

小牛犢稚嫩的叫聲；

不再聽到火爐架上水壺的輕唱；

不再聽到曾經安撫他心靈的歌謠；

還有那灰鼠繞著箱子，

圍著燕麥片箱子跳躍不已的聲響。

因為他來了，人間的孩子，

到荒野和沼澤裡來了，

和精靈手牽著手，

這個世界哭聲太多，可你不懂。

Away with us he's going,

The solemn-eyed:

He'll hear no more the lowing

Of the calves on the warm hillside

Or the kettle on the hob

Sing peace into his breast,

Or see the brown mice bob

Round and round the oatmeal-chest.

For he comes, the human child,

To the waters and the wild

With a faery, hand in hand,

From a world more full of weeping than he can understand.

印度人致所愛／

小島還在晨曦中酣睡，

沉寂從碩大的樹枝間瀝出；

滑軟的草坪上，孔雀正翩然起舞，

樹梢上，一隻鸚鵡在不停搖盪，

對著碧海中自己的身影嘯鳴不止。

我們將孤單的船泊在這裡，

手攜著手，款步依依，向前暢遊，

唇貼著唇，溫柔體貼，喃喃低語；

我們沿著草坪，順著沙丘

低訴著，那喧囂的塵世何等遙遠。

The Indian to His Love

The island dreams under the dawn

And great boughs drop tranquillity;

The peahens dance on a smooth lawn,

A parrot sways upon a tree,

Raging at his own image in the enamelled sea.

Here we will moor our lonely ship

And wander ever with woven hands,

Murmuring softly lip to lip,

Along the grass, along the sands,

Murmuring how far away are the unquiet lands:

低訴著，我們這遠離塵囂的人，

是如何遠遠隱匿在靜謐的樹下，

我們的愛情長成一顆印度的明星，

化為一顆燃燒之心的流星，

那心裡有閃爍的潮汐，

有疾馳的翅膀。

沉重的枝頭和光彩奪目、哀歎百日的鴿子，

絮絮著我們死後靈魂又要怎樣飄零，

那時，黃昏的沉寂將撒滿羽毛的道路遮蓋，

海水慵懶的粼光邊足跡依稀。

How we alone of mortals are

Hid under quiet boughs apart,

While our love grows an Indian star,

A meteor of the burning heart,

One with the tide that gleams, the wings that gleam and dart,

The heavy boughs, the burnished dove

That moans and sighs a hundred days:

How when we die our shades may rove,

When eve has hushed thc feathered ways,

With vapoury footsole among the water's drowsy blaze.

經柳園而下／

經柳園而下，我曾遇上我的愛，

她走過柳園，纖足雪白。

她要我自然地去愛，就像樹木吐出新芽。

但我，年少愚笨，不曾聽從。

在河邊的田野裡，我曾和我的愛人駐足，

在我傾靠的肩上，她放下雪白的手。

她要我自然地生活，就像堤堰長出青草；

但那時，我年少愚笨，如今淚濕衣衫。

Down by the Salley Gardens

Down by the salley gardens my love and I did meet;

She passed the salley gardens with little snow-white feet.

She bid me take love easy, as the leaves grow on the tree;

But I, being young and foolish, with her would not agree.

In a field by the river my love and I did stand,

And on my leaning shoulder she laid her snow-white hand.

She bid me take life easy, as the grass grows on the weirs;

But I was young and foolish, and now am full of tears.

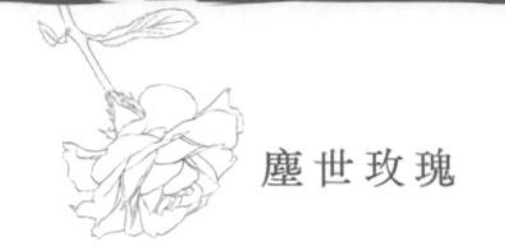

塵世玫瑰／

誰曾想像過美如夢一般地消隱？

就因為那紅唇凝聚著所有悲哀的驕傲，

悲哀著不會再有新的奇蹟降臨，

特洛伊早在萬丈火焰中毀滅，

尤斯納的兒女們也無一存活。

我們和這痛苦的世界一起，

芸芸眾生的靈魂消逝於動搖與讓步，

宛如蒼涼冬日江河裡奔騰的流水，

如同泡沫般泯滅的星空，

僅存著一張孤獨的面容。

天使啊，鞠躬吧，在你們昏暗的住處，

當你們誕生之前，或心臟跳動之前，

那位疲憊的仁者，在座前徘徊，

他將這世界變作青草大道，

鋪開在她浪跡的雙足之前。

The Rose of the World

Who dreamed that beauty passes like a dream?

For these red lips, with all their mournful pride,

Mournful that no new wonder may betide,

Troy passed away in one high funeral gleam,

And Usna's children died.

We and the labouring world are passing by:

Amid men's souls, that waver and give place,

Like the pale waters in their wintry race,

Under the passing stars, foam of the sky,

Lives on this lonely face.

Bow down, archangels, in your dim abode:

Before you were, or any hearts to beat,

Weary and kind one lingered by His seat;

He made the world to be a grassy road

Before her wandering feet.

茵尼斯弗利島／

我將起身離去，去茵尼斯弗利島：
用樹枝和泥土，在那裡築起小屋，
我要種九壟豆角，為蜜蜂做個小巢，
獨居於幽境裡，聽群峰歌唱。

於是我會享有安靜，安靜緩緩滴零，
從晨曦的面紗到蟋蟀歌唱的世界；
午夜一絲微火，中午紫霞燃燒，
暮色裡，無數紅雀的翅膀漫天飛舞。

我將起身離去，因為我總是聽到，
湖水日夜輕輕拍打著堤岸；
我站在公路上，或在灰色的人行道間，
那濤聲卻拍打在我的心底深處。

The Lake Isle of Innisfree

I will arise and go now, and go to Innisfree,

And a small cabin build there, of clay and wattles made:

Nine bean rows will I have there, a hive for the honey bee,

And live alone in the bee-loud glade.

And I shall have some peace there, for peace

comes dropping slow,

Dropping from the veils of the morning to

where the cricket sings;

There midnight's all a glimmer, and noon a purple glow,

And evening full of the linnet's wings.

I will arise and go now, for always night and day

I hear lake water lapping with low sounds

by the shore;

While I stand on the roadway, or on the

pavements grey,

I hear it in the deep heart's core.

愛的憂傷／

一隻麻雀在屋簷下聒噪，

皎潔的月亮，璀璨的繁星，

和樹葉優美和諧的歌唱，

掩飾著人類的影像和哭聲。

一位憂傷的紅唇少女顯露面容，

仿佛整個偉大的世界也噙滿了淚水，

如奧德修斯和他的船隊遭受的厄運，

如普裡阿摩率隊殉城的驕傲；

顯現升起來了，在這喧鬧的屋簷，

空曠的天穹裡上升的明月，

樹葉唱起憂傷的歌，

只組成了人類的影像和哭聲。

The Sorrow of Love

The brawling of a sparrow in the eaves,
The brilliant moon and all the milky sky,
And all that famous harmony of leaves,
Had blotted out man's image and his cry.

A girl arose that had red mournful lips
And seemed the greatness of the world in tears,
Doomed like Odysseus and the labouring ships
And proud as Priam murdered with his peers;

Arose, and on the instant clamorous eaves,
A climbing moon upon an empty sky,
And all that lamentation of the leaves,
Could but compose man's image and his cry.

當你老了／

當你老了，兩鬢斑白，睡意沉沉，
倦坐在爐邊時，請取下這部詩作，
慢慢誦頌，追憶那當年的眼神，
神色柔和，倒影深深。
多少人曾愛慕你青春嫵媚的身影，
愛慕你的容顏出自真情或者假意，
卻唯獨一人愛你那聖潔的靈魂，
愛你日漸衰老的臉上愁苦的風霜；

在熾熱的爐火旁邊，你彎下身軀，
淒然地低聲哀訴，愛情如何逝去，
在頭頂上的群峰之巔漫步閒遊，
將他的面容隱沒於繁星之間。

When You Are Old

When you are old and grey and full of sleep,

And nodding by the fire, take down this book,

And slowly read, and dream of the soft look

Your eyes had once, and of their shadows deep,

How many loved your moments of glad grace,

And loved your beauty will love false or true;

But one man loved the pilgrim soul in you,

And loved the sorrows of your changing face.

And bending down beside the glowing bars

Murmur, a little sadly, how love fled

And paced upon the mountains overhead

And hid his face amid a crowd of stars.

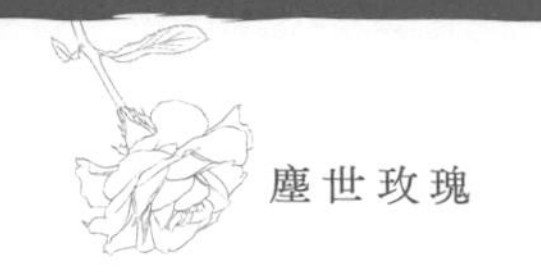

誰和費古斯一同前往／

誰願與費古斯同車前去，

穿過那濃林密織的蔭影，

到平坦的海邊，翩翩起舞？

年輕人，揚起你棕黃的眉頭，

姑娘，抬起你溫柔的眼皮，

滿懷希望吧，別再擔心害怕。

不再孤獨，不再沉思，

不再深思愛情苦澀的神祕，

因為費古斯駕馭著黃銅戰車，

統治著森林的蔭翳，

雄渾海洋的雪白胸膛，及

錯亂有致的滿天繁星。

When You Are Old

Who will go drive with Fergus now,

And pierce the deep wood's woven shade,

And dance upon the level shore?

Young man, lift up your russet brow,

And lift your tender eyelids, maid,

And brood on hopes and fears no more.

And no more turn aside and brood

Upon Love's bitter mystery,

For Fergus rules the brazen cars,

And rules the shadows of the wood,

And the white breast of the dim sea

And all dishevelled wandering stars.

愛人述說著他心中的玫瑰花／

醜陋破碎的萬物，殘缺古老的萬物，
路邊孩子的哭喊，緩行馬車的尖嘯，
耕夫沉重的腳步，濺起冬日的泥土，
都在詆毀著你的形象——在我心中綻開的那朵玫瑰花。

醜陋的萬物，一錯再錯，無以言表；
我渴望重塑世界，然後獨坐在綠色山丘上，
守望著嶄新的大地、天空與海洋，如同一只金匣，

因為我夢著你的形象——在我心中綻開的那朵玫瑰花。

The Lover Tells of the Rose in His Heart

ALL things uncomely and broken, all things worn out and old,
The cry of a child by the roadway, the creak of a lumbering cart,
The heavy steps of the ploughman, splashing the wintry mould,
Are wronging your image that blossoms a rose in the deeps of
my heart.

The wrong of unshapely things is a wrong too great to be told;
I hunger to build them anew and sit on a green knoll apart,
With the earth and the sky and the water, re—made, like a
casket of gold.
For my dreams of your image that blossoms a rose in the deeps
of my heart.

魚／

雖然你躲藏在蒼白的潮起潮落中，

在那月已西落之時，

可人們總是會知曉

我是如何將漁網撒出，

你又是如何無數次地翻跳，

那些纖細的銀線，

又認為你殘酷無情，

並用尖刻的話語把你責備。

The Fish

Although you hide in the ebb and flow

Of the pale tide when the moon has set,

The people of coming days will know

About the casting out of my net,

And how you have leaped times out of mind

Over the little silver cords,

And think that you were hard and unkind,

And blame you with many bitter words.

步入暮色／

在一個疲倦的時代裡，一顆疲倦的心，

擺脫了那張是非織成的網。

歡笑吧，心，再一次在灰暗的暮色中；

歎息吧，心，再一次在黎明的露珠中。

你的祖國愛爾蘭永保生機，

露珠永遠晶瑩，暮色永遠朦朧；

儘管你失去了希望，並且愛已枯萎——

這一切在誹謗的火焰中燃燒殆盡。

來吧，心，那裡層巒疊翠，

因為太陽和月亮，幽谷和樹林，

還有小河和溪流，有著神祕的

兄弟之情，按著它們的意志前行。

上帝佇立著，婉轉地奏響他那孤獨的號角，

時空總在不斷飛逝；

愛情還沒有灰暗的暮色那樣美好多情，

希望還不如黎明的露珠那樣和藹可親。

Into the Twilight

Out-worn heart, in a time out-worn,

Come clear of the nets of wrong and right;

Laugh, heart, again in the gray twilight;

Sigh, heart, again in the dew of the morn.

Thy mother Eire is always young,

Dew ever shining and twilight gray,

Though hope fall from thee or love decay

Burning in fires of a slanderous tongue.

Come, heart, where hill is heaped upon hill,

For there the mystical brotherhood

Of hollow wood and the hilly wood

And the changing moon work out their will.

And God stands winding his lonely horn;

And Time and World are ever in flight,

And love is less kind than the gray twilight,

And hope is less dear than the dew of the morn.

流浪者安格斯之歌／

我走出門，走到榛樹林中，

因為我心頭有一團火，

我砍一根榛子樹枝，削成釣竿，

又用線縛上一顆小漿果；

當到粉白蛾子飛舞的時候，

粉蛾似的星星也閃現在天際之時，

我把漿果拋入小溪，

釣起一條銀光閃閃的小鱒魚。

當我把小鱒魚放在地板上，

轉身去把火爐生旺，

但有什麼東西在地上沙沙作響，

哦，一個人正叫著我的名字：

原來蹲魚變成了光彩奪目的姑娘，

鬢邊簪著蘋果花，

她喊著我的名字就跑開，

消失在晨曦熹微中。

The Song of Wandering Aengus

I went out to the hazel wood,

Because a fire was in my head,

And cut and peeled a hazel wand,

And hooked a berry to a thread;

And when white moths were on the wing,

And moth-like stars were flickering out,

I dropped the berry in a stream

And caught a little silver trout.

When I had laid it on the floor

I went to blow the fire a-flame,

But something rustled on the floor,

And someone called me by my name:

It had become a glimmering girl

With apple blossom in her hair

Who called me by my name and ran

And faded through the brightening air.

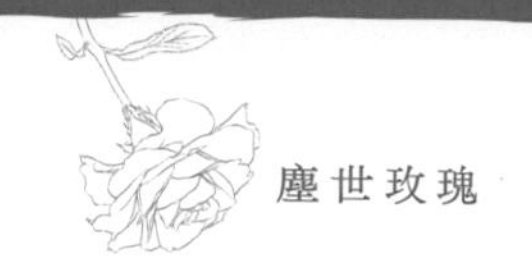

雖然我已經流浪到老，

我還要跋涉千山萬水，

尋覓她的蹤跡，

親吻她的嘴唇，握緊她的雙手；

漫步在花兒斑駁的草地，

摘著月亮的銀蘋果，

摘著太陽的金蘋果，

摘著，摘著，直到天荒地老。

Though I am old with wandering

Through hollow lands and hilly lands,

I will find out where she has gone,

And kiss her lips and take her hands;

And walk among long dappled grass,

And pluck till time and times are done,

The silver apples of the moon,

The golden apples of the sun.

女人的心／

哦，那狹小的房間於我何用，

儘管房間裡充斥著祈禱與祝福；

他將我喚出並隱入暮色，

將我的胸與他的胸緊緊相貼。

哦，母親的關懷於我何用，

儘管我住在家中安全又溫暖；

我那濃密的頭髮宛若花開，

已足以使我們抵擋暴風驟雨。

哦，他那濃密的頭髮，清澈的眼睛

使我從此不再顧慮生死，

我的心與他溫暖的心緊緊依偎，

我們的氣息與生命相通相融。

The Heart of the Woman

O What to me the little room

That was brimmed up with prayer and rest;

He bade me out into the gloom,

And my breast lies upon his breast.

O what to me my mother's care,

The house where I was safe and warm;

The shadowy blossom of my hair

Will hide us from the bitter storm.

O hiding hair and dewy eyes,

I am no more with life and death,

My heart upon his warm heart lies,

My breath is mixed into his breath.

戀人爲失戀的傷悼／

白皙容顏，秀髮密髻，纖手安詳，

我曾有過一個美麗的朋友，

夢中憶起往昔的絕望

將在這新的戀情中終結。

一天，她看透我的心事，

見你的影子依然，揮之不去：

她慟哭著，遠遠離開。

The Lover Mourns for the Loss of Love

Pale brows, still hands and dim hair,

I had a beautiful friend

And dreamed that the old despair

Would end in love in the end:

She looked in my heart one day

And saw your image was there;

She has gone weeping away.

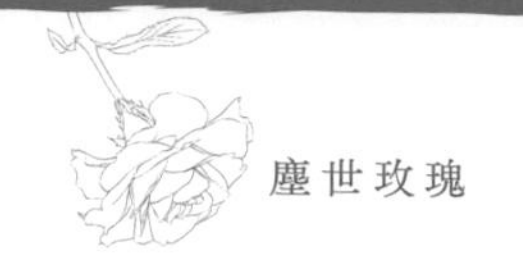

他要他的愛人安靜／

我聽見那幻影般的馬群，鬃毛抖顫，

蹄聲沉重而喧嘩，眼睛閃爍著白光；

北方在它們頭頂展開匍匐緊貼的夜色，

東方在破曉之前急忙展開隱藏的歡樂，

西方流著蒼白的眼淚，悲泣著飄逝；

南方向大地傾注玫瑰樣深紅的火，

呵，虛幻的榮華，希望，夢想和沒有止境的欲望，

深深的泥潭將那帶來災難的馬群埋葬；

親愛的，微閉雙眼，讓你的心

緊貼我的心，把你那秀髮垂灑在我的胸上，

讓靜謐深沉的暮色吞咽愛的孤獨時光，

吞沒飄動的鬃毛和馬蹄的震盪。

He Bids His Beloved Be at Peace

I HEAR the Shadowy Horses, their long manes a-shake,

Their hoofs heavy with tumult, their eyes glimmering white;

The North unfolds above them clinging, creeping night,

The East her hidden joy before the morning break,

The West weeps in pale dew and sighs passing away,

The South is pouring down roses of crimson fire:

O vanity of Sleep, Hope, Dream, endless Desire,

The Horses of Disaster plunge in the heavy clay:

Beloved, let your eyes half close, and your heart beat

Over my heart, and your hair fall over my breast,

Drowning love's lonely hour in deep twilight of rest,

And hiding their tossing manes and their tumultuous feet.

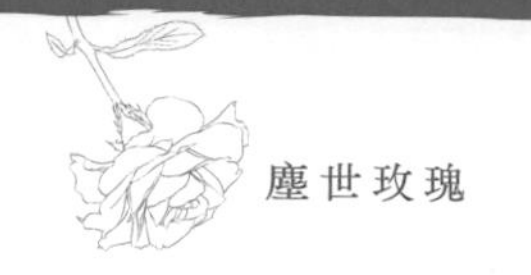

他想起了那忘卻的美／

當我的雙臂緊緊環抱著你時，

我把我的心緊貼那片美麗——

那早已從這世上消逝了的美麗。

那頂在潰逃的軍隊中被皇帝

扔進汙池裡的珍貴皇冠，

那些愛幻想的貴婦們在絨布上

用銀絲線織出、把兇殘

的蛀蟲們養肥的愛情故事，

在往昔的日子裡，那些曾

簪在貴婦秀髮裡的玫瑰。

He Remembers Forgotten Beauty

When my arms wrap you round I press

My heart upon the loveliness

That has long faded from the world;

The jewelled crowns that kings have hurled

In shadowy pools, when armies fled;

The love-tales wrought with silken thread

By dreaming ladies upon cloth

That has made fat the murderous moth;

The roses that of old time were

Woven by ladies in their hair,

走過神聖的走廊時，貴婦們

手中都捧著露珠般冰冷的百合，

那裡，玫瑰香灰暗的煙雲悠悠升起，

唯有上帝的眼睛不被迷閉。

因為這白晰的酥胸和依戀的雙手，

均來自一個充滿夢幻的土地，

一個比它更充滿夢幻的時刻；

當你在親吻間，渴望不已，

我聽到白色的美神也不斷渴望著。

為著那樣的時刻：一切必似露水消逝，

只剩下火焰上的火焰，海洋下的海洋，

和王座上的王座，那裡半睡半醒，

帝王們把劍枕在鐵一樣的膝上，

她沉思著她那高傲而孤寂的神祕。

The dew-cold lilies ladies bore

Through many a sacred corridor

Where such grey clouds of incense rose

That only God's eyes did not close:

For that pale breast and lingering hand

Come from a more dream-heavy land,

A more dream-heavy hour than this;

And when you sigh from kiss to kiss

I hear white Beauty sighing, too,

For hours when all must fade like dew.

But flame on flame, and deep on deep,

Throne over throne where in half sleep,

Their swords upon their iron knees,

Brood her high lonely mysteries.

詩人致所愛／

我用充滿敬意的手給你帶來

我無窮無盡的夢幻書籍，

被激情折磨得蒼白的女人，

就像潮水磨得沙子灰而微紅；

從蒼白的時間之火中傳出了

古老的號角聲，但更古老的是我的心

因無窮無盡的夢而蒼白的女人，

為你，我獻上熱烈而多情的音韻。

A Poet to His Beloved

I bring you with reverent hands

The books of my numberless dreams,

White woman that passion has worn

As the tide wears the dove-grey sands,

And with heart more old than the horn

That is brimmed from the pale fire of time:

White woman with numberless dreams,

I bring you my passionate rhyme.

他獻給他愛人的詩／

用金色髮卡束緊你的頭髮，

束緊每一縷散亂的頭髮，

我讓我的心寫下這拙劣的詩文，

編寫它們，夜以繼日，

從過去的搏鬥，昔日的抗爭，

譜寫出一種憂傷的情懷。

你僅需抬起一隻玉手，

綰起那長長的秀髮，發出一聲歎息，

男人們的心喲，便會跳躍燃燒。

暗淡的沙灘上白浪如燭火，

微露的夜空繁星閃耀，

只為了照亮你的纖足。

He Gives His Beloved Certain Rhymes

Fasten your hair with a golden pin,

And bind up every wandering tress;

I bade my heart build these poor rhymes:

It worked at them, day out, day in,

Building a sorrowful loveliness

Out of the battles of old times.

You need but lift a pearl-palc hand,

And bind up your long hair and sigh;

And all men's hearts must burn and beat;

And candle-like foam on the dim sand,

And stars climbing the dew-dropping sky,

Live but to light your passing feet.

便帽與戲鈴／

弄臣漫步在花園，

花園早已靜寂無聲；

他命靈魂悄然離去，

飄落在她的窗櫺；

著藍衣的靈魂遵命而去，

當貓頭鷹開始長嚎短吟；

它早已變得口齒伶俐，

因想到她那輕盈的足跡；

但年輕的王后不願聆聽，

她身披淺白的睡袍起身，

伸手關閉沉重的窗櫺，

用道道插銷把其閂緊。

The Cap and Bells

The jester walked in the garden:

The garden had fallen still;

He bade his soul rise upward

And stand on her window-sill.

It rose in a straight blue garment,

When owls began to call:

It had grown wise-tongucd by thinking

Of a quiet and light footfall;

But the young queen would not listen;

She rose in her pale night-gown;

She drew in the heavy casement

And pushed the latches down.

他命令他的心去與她相會，

當貓頭鷹已不再嚎鳴，

心兒裹著紅衣顫抖出門，

哼著歌曲穿過她的門庭。

它的歌聲早已變得甜美，

因為夢見花一樣飄拂的髮鬢；

可她從妝台拾起繡扇，

拂散了盪氣迴腸的歌聲。

He bade his heart go to her,

When the owls called out no more;

In a red and quivering garment

It sang to her through the door.

It had grown sweet-tongued by dreaming

Of a flutter of flower-like hair;

But she took up her fan from the table

And waved it off on the air.

他暗想：「我有便帽和戲鈴，

我要奉送給她再結束生命。」

當東方漸漸露出晨曦，

他把贈物留在她必經的幽徑。

她摟住便帽和戲鈴，

垂下一頭秀髮猶如烏雲，

輕啟朱唇唱起情歌，

直到天空閃出點點繁星。

她打開門扉，推開窗葉，

讓那心兒和靈魂進了房門，

她右手托起鮮紅的心兒，

左手飛來晶藍的靈魂。

它們似蟋蟀唧唧和鳴，

悄聲細語甜美又動聽，

她的秀髮如花兒一樣盤起，

她的腳下鋪滿了愛的寧靜。

"I have cap and bells," he pondered,

"I will send them to her and die";

And when the morning whitened

He left them where she went by.

She laid them upon her bosom,

Under a cloud of her hair,

And her red lips sang them a love-song

Till stars grew out of the air.

She opened her door and her window,

And the heart and the soul came through,

To her right hand came the red one,

To her left hand came the blue.

They set up a noise like crickets,

A chattering wise and sweet,

And her hair was a folded flower

And the quiet of love in her feet.

他描述情人幽谷／

夢中我站在幽谷之中，四周一片歎息，

因為幸福的戀人正成雙成對從我站立的地方經過。

我昔日的情人悄然出現在林間，

白雲般的眼簾低垂在夢幻般的雙眸前。

在夢中我呼喊，啊，女人們，讓年輕的男子

將頭枕在你們膝上，並用你們的秀髮把他們眼睛遮掩，

否則回憶起她的容顏，就覺得無更美可言，

直到這世間的幽谷深澗都已消失殆盡。

He Tells of a Valley Full of Lovers

I dreamel that I stood in a valley, and amid sighs,

For happy lovers passed two by two where I stood;

And I dreamed my lost love came stealthily out of the wood

With her cloud-pale eyelids falling on dream-dimmed eyes:

I cried in my dream, O women, bid the young men lay

Their heads on your knees, and drown their eyes with your fair,

Or remembering hers they will find no other face fair

Till all thc valleys of the world have been withered away.

他描述絕倫的美／

哦，那聖潔似雲的眼簾，夢幻般朦朧的雙眸，

詩人們夜以繼日奮筆疾書，

在韻律中去成就一種絕倫的美，

卻被一個女人的凝視輕易擊潰，

被蒼穹裡悠閒的星辰輕易推翻。

因此，當露水滴落睡意之時，

我的心為之傾倒，直至上帝燃盡時間，

在那閒適的群星和你的面前。

He Tells of the Perfect Beauty

O cloud-pale eyelids, dream-dimmed eyes,

The poets labouring all their days

To build a perfect beauty in rhyme

Are overthrown by a woman's gaze

And by the unlabouring brood of the skies:

And therefore my heart will bow, when dew

Is dropping sleep, until God burn time,

Before the unlabouring stars and you.

隱祕的玫瑰／

遙遠的、隱祕的、不可褻瀆的玫瑰啊，

在關鍵的時刻擁抱我吧；在那裡，

那些曾在聖墓中或者在酒車裡

尋找你的人，生活在破滅了的夢的騷動

和混亂之外；深深地

在蒼白的眼瞼之中，睡意慵懶而沉重，

人們稱之為美。你那巨大的葉子

包裹著古人的鬍鬚，和光榮的三聖人獻來的

紅寶石與金子；還有那個帝王，他

目睹釘穿了的手和接骨木的十字架，

在德魯德的幻想中站起，使火炬暗淡，

最後從夢幻中醒來又死去，還有他，

他曾遇見范德在火焰般的露水中走向遠方，

走在風兒從來無法經過的灰色海岸上，

於是他在一吻之下丟掉了愛瑪和天下。

The Secret Rose

Far-off, most secret, and inviolate Rose,

Enfold me in my hour of hours; where those

Who sought thee in the Holy Sepulchre,

Or in the wine-vat, dwell beyond the stir

And tumult of defeated dreams; and deep

Among pale eyelids, heavy with the sleep

Men have named beauty. Thy great leaves enfold

The ancient beards, the helms of ruby and gold

Of the crowned Magi; and the king whose eyes

Saw the pierced Hands and Rood of elder rise

In Druid vapour and make the torches dim;

Till vain frenzy awoke and he died; and him

Who met Fand walking among flaming dew

By a grey shore where the wind never blew,

And lost the world and Emer for a kiss;

還有他，他曾把神祇從要塞裡驅趕出來，

直到第一百個早晨開花，姹紫嫣紅，

他飽賞美景，又在埋著同伴的墳邊哭泣；

還有他，那個自豪的、做夢的帝王，把王冠

和悲傷拋開，把吟游詩人和小丑叫來，

他們曾居住在密林裡酒漬斑斑的流浪者中間；

還有他，賣了耕田、房屋和所有的物品，

多少年來，在陸地和島上尋找，

最後他終於找到了，悲喜交集，

這樣一個光彩奪目、容顏照人的女孩，

午夜，人們用她的一綹頭髮照著把稻穀打

一小綹偷來的頭髮。我也等待著

颶風般襲來的愛恨交織的時刻。

何時，星星在天空被風吹得四散，

就像鐵匠鋪裡冒出的火星，然後黯淡？

顯然屬於你的時代已經到來，颶風猛刮，

遙遠的、隱祕的、不可褻瀆的玫瑰花呢？

And him who drove the gods out of their liss,

And till a hundred morns had flowered red

Feasted, and wept the barrows of his dead;

And the proud dreaming king who flung the crown

And sorrow away, and calling bard and clown

Dwelt among wine-stained wanderers in deep woods:

And him who sold tillage, and house, and goods,

And sought through lands and islands numberless years,

Until he found, with laughter and with tears,

A woman of so shining loveliness

That men threshed corn at midnight by a tress,

A little stolen tress. I, too, await

The hour of thy great wind of love and hate.

When shall the stars be blown about the sky,

Like the sparks blown out of a smithy, and die?

Surely thine hour has come, thy great wind blows,

Far-off, most secret, and inviolate Rose?

他希望能得到天堂中的錦繡／

倘若我能得到天堂中的錦繡，

織滿了金色的和銀色的光彩，

有著湛藍的夜色與潔白的晝光

以及黃昏和黎明朦朧的光芒，

我願把這塊錦繡鋪展在你的腳下——

可是我窮，除了夢，一無所有；

於是我把我的夢鋪展到了你的腳下，

輕一點啊，因為你踩著的是我的夢。

He Wishes for the Cloths of Heaven

Had I the heavens' embroidered cloths,

Enwrought with golden and silver light,

The blue and the dim and the dark cloths

Of night and light and the half-light,

I would spread the cloths under your feet:

But I, being poor, have only my dreams;

I have spread my dreams under your feet;

Tread softly because you tread on my dreams.

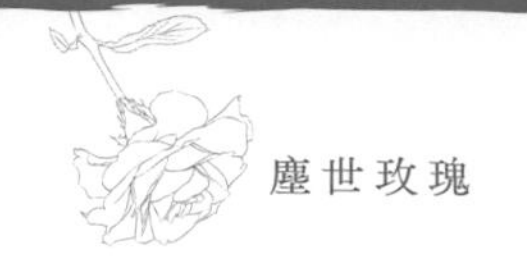

決不要獻上整顆心／

決不要獻上整顆心，因為愛情

在那些熱情洋溢狂熱的女人心裡，

如果有確定的把握，似乎就不值一想，

但她們做夢也沒想到，

愛情在一次次親吻中凋零；

一切可愛的事物不過是

短暫、友愛、夢幻般的歡欣。

啊，決不要貿然獻上整顆心，

因為那些女人極盡花言巧語，

掏出心窩只是逢場作戲，

但誰又能玩得更精彩，如果

愛到聵聾、暗啞、盲目？

這些經歷過，如今他認清了所有的代價，

因為他獻出了而又喪失了整顆心。

Never Give All the Heart

Never give all the heart, for love
Will hardly seem worth thinking of
To passionate women if it seem
Certain, and they never dream
That it fades out from kiss to kiss;
For everything that's lovely is
But a brief, dreamy. Kind delight.
O never give the heart outright,
For they, for all smooth lips can say,
Have given their hearts up to the play.
And who could play it well enough
If deaf and dumb and blind with love?
He that made this knows all the cost,
For he gave all his heart and lost.

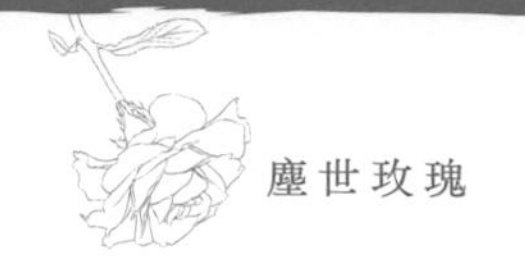

亞當的詛咒／

我們聚坐，在炎夏的盡頭，

那美麗溫柔的女子——你的好友，

還有你我，一起談論詩歌，

我說：「一行詩花上幾個時辰，

可如果沒有 那迸發的靈感，

我們織了又拆，都是徒勞，

還不如雙膝跪地，

去擦擦地板，或敲敲石子，

像一個年老的乞丐，無論風吹雨淋；

因為絕妙的音韻

比這些都繁瑣，

就要被嘮叨的銀行家、

校長和牧師們這些塵世的殉道者們

認為是遊手好閒之輩。」

Adam's Curse

We sat together at one summer's end,
That beautiful mild woman, your close friend,
And you and I, and talked of poetry.
I said, "A line will take us hours maybe;
Yet if it does not seem a moment's thought,
Our stitching and unstitching has been naught.
Better go down upon your marrow-bones
And scrub a kitchen pavement, or break stones
Like an old pauper, in all kinds of weather;
For to articulate sweet sounds together
Is to work harder than all these, and yet
Be thought an idler by the noisy set
Of bankers, schoolmasters, and clergymen
The martyrs call the world."

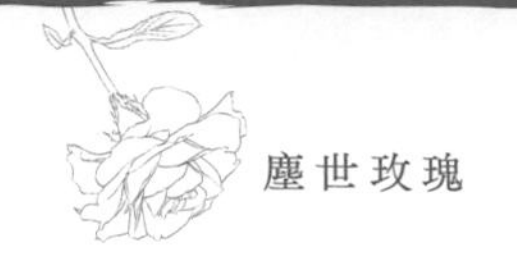

於是

那美麗溫柔的女子，應聲——

這嗓音低沉而甜美，

讓人感到心中隱隱作痛：

「身為一個女人就該知道，

雖然學校裡不把這個當成話題，

我們卻必須努力去追求美麗。」

我說：「是啊，自亞當墮落以來，

任何美好的事物都要消耗大量精力，

戀人們曾經認為，愛情

理應由高雅的殷勤營造，

他們歎氣，擺出一副博學的面容，

從精美的古典中旁徵博引，

如今看來，無聊至極。」

And thereupon

That beautiful mild woman for whose sake

There's many a one shall find out all heartache

On finding that her voice is sweet and low

Replied, "To be born woman is to know -

Although they do not talk of it at school -

That we must labour to be beautiful."

I said, "It's certain there is no fine thing

Since Adam's fall but needs much labouring.

There have been lovers who thought love should be

So much compounded of high courtesy

That they would sigh and quote with learned looks

precedents out of beautiful old books;

Yet now it seems an idle trade enough."

我們聚坐，因提到了愛情而靜默，

看夕陽燃盡了最後一縷光影，

在蒼穹顫抖著的藍綠之光中，

如貝的殘月高高懸掛，

在歲月的潮水中起起落落，

在星辰的明滅中消損殆盡。

我有一個想法，只能說給你聽：

你奪目的容顏令我神往，

用古老愛情的高雅方式，

曾經那般幸福，但我們都已改變——

疲憊的心此刻正如那消損的殘月。

We sat grown quiet at the name of love;

We saw the last embers of daylight die,

And in the trembling blue-green of the sky

A moon, worn as if it had been a shell

Washed by time's waters as they rose and fell

About the stars and broke in days and years.

I had a thought for no one's but your ears:

That you were beautiful, and that I strove

To love you in the old high way of love;

That it had all seemed happy, and yet we'd grown

As weary-hearted as that hollow moon.

水中自我欣賞的老人／

我聽到那些年邁的老人說，

「一切都在改變，

我們一個接一個地死去。」

他們手如雀爪，雙膝

似水邊的老荊棘樹枝，

疤節生累累。

我聽到那些年邁的老人說，

「美好的一切終將逝去，

就像這流水。」

The Old Men Admiring Them-selves in the Water

I HEARD the old, old men say,

"Everything alters,

And one by one we drop away."

They had hands like claws, and their knees

Were twisted like the old thorn-trees

By the waters.

I heard the old, old men say,

"All that's beautiful drifts away

Like the waters."

聽人安慰的愚蠢／

昨天，一個總是那麼善良的人說起：

「你深愛的那個人，髮中已有了銀絲，

小小的陰影佈滿了她的眼圈，

時間只能使人更容易變聰明，

儘管現在似乎不可能，因此

你所需要的只是耐心。」

可我的心在哭喊：「不，

我不會得到一絲安慰，即使一點點，

時間也能使她越來越美；

因為她的華貴風姿，

爐火在她身旁跳動，當她跳動時，

爐火更為旺盛。哦，她絕無這些瑕疵，

即使當狂野夏日來臨。」

心啊，心喲！只要她願意轉回身，

你就會知道聽人安慰有多愚蠢。

The Folly of Being Comforted

ONE that is ever kind said yesterday:

"Your well-beloved's hair has threads of grey,

And little shadows come about her eyes;

Time can but make it easier to be wise

Though now it seems impossible, and so

All that you need is patience."

Heart cries, "No,

I have not a crumb of comfort, not a grain.

Time can but make her beauty over again:

Because of that great nobleness of hers

The fire that stirs about her, when she stirs,

Burns but more clearly. O she had not these ways

When all the wild Summer was in her gaze."

Heart! O heart! if she'd but turn her head,

You'd know the folly of being comforted.

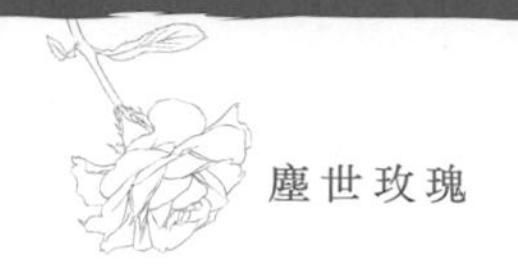

這些是雲霞／

這些是落日——那闔上他憤怒的

眼睛的君王——周圍的雲霞。

弱者企圖插手於強者的作為，

直到那高高的權貴翻了個身，

和諧過後是一片混亂，

一切都處於一個共同的高度。

所以，朋友，如果你跑完偉大的賽程，

所有這些事情來臨，更因為這個緣故

你的豐功偉績成就了自己的光榮，

儘管你歎息是為了孩子們：

這些是落日——那闔上他憤怒的

眼睛的君王——周圍的雲霞。

These Are the Clouds

These are the clouds about the fallen sun,

The majesty that shuts his burning eye:

The weak lay hand on what the strong has done,

Till that be tumbled that was lifted high

And discord follow upon unison,

And all things at one common level lie.

And therefore, friend, if your great race were run

And these things came, So much the more thereby

Have you made greatness your companion,

Although it be for children that you sigh:

These are the clouds about the fallen sun,

The majesty that shuts his burning eye.

一位友人的疾病／

疾病帶給我這種

想法，放在他的天平上：

我又何須驚恐不安？

雖然烈火早已燃盡整個

世界，彷彿煤炭一般，

但如今我看到天平的那頭

是一個人的靈魂？

A Friend's Illness

Sickness brought me this

Thought, in that scale of his:

Why should I be dismayed

Though flame had burned the whole

World, as it were a coal,

Now I have seen it weighed

Against a soul?

棕色的便士／

我低聲絮語：「我太年輕，」

轉念又一想：「我還不夠成熟。」

因此我拋出一枚便士，

看看我能否得到愛情。

「去愛吧，去愛吧，年輕人，

如果那個姑娘年輕又漂亮。」

啊，便士，便士，我那棕色的便士，

我陶醉於她那美麗的髮圈。

哦，愛情是件叫人琢磨不透的事，

沒有誰足夠聰明

能夠去破解愛情的秘笈，

因為他總在沉思愛情的神祕，

直到那星星都已隱去，

月亮也躲進了烏雲裡。

啊，便士，便士，我那棕色的便士，

開始戀愛從來不嫌早。

Brown Penny

I whispered, "I am too young,"

And then, "I am old enough";

Wherefore I threw a penny

To find out if I might love.

"Go and love, go and love, young man,

If the lady be young and fair."

Ah, penny, brown penny, brown penny,

I am looped in the loops of her hair.

O love is the crooked thing,

There is nobody wise enough

To find out all that is in it,

For he would be thinking of love

Till the stars had run away

And the shadows eaten the moon.

Ah, penny, brown penny, brown penny,

One cannot begin it too soon.

致一個幽魂／

如果你曾經重遊故城，淡淡的幽魂，

每當凝視你那高聳的紀念碑，

(我想知道修碑的人是否得到了報酬)

或幸福地想著，當時光流逝，

去啜飲遼闊的海洋中帶著的鹹味氣息，

灰色的海鷗在人群中飛來飛去，

荒涼的屋脊披上晚霞的莊嚴之時：

讓這些使你滿足然後重新逝去；

因為他們還在玩弄舊時的把戲。

To a Shade

If you have revisited the town, thin Shade,

Whether to look upon your monument

(I wonder if the builder has been paid)

Or happier-thoughted when the day is spent

To drink of that salt breath out of the sea

When grey gulls flit about instead of men,

And the gaunt houses put on majesty:

Let these content you and be gone again;

For they are at their old tricks yet.

一個與你有著

同樣的獻身激情的人——他們不會知道，

他強健的雙手帶來的那一切

會使他們的子孫思想崇高，

感情甜美，就像高貴的血液

在他們體內流動。可他遭到放逐，

他的辛苦只換來了重重侮辱，

而他的慷慨，都給他帶來羞愧恥辱；

你的仇敵有一張邪惡的嘴，

唆使群狗去撕咬他。

走吧，不得安寧的流浪者，

用格拉斯奈文的被單圍住你的頭，

直到灰塵不再進入你的雙耳；

現在不是你呼吸海洋氣息的時刻，

也不是你在角落偷偷傾聽的時光。

在你去世之前，已有夠多的傷心悲苦，

去吧，去吧，躺在墳墓裡你會更加太平。

A man
Of your own passionate serving kind who had brought
In his full hands what, had they only known,
Had given their children's children loftier thought,
Sweeter emotion, working in their veins
Like gentle blood, has been driven from the place,
And insult heaped upon him for his pains,
And for his open-handedness, disgrace;
Your enemy, an old foul mouth, had set
The pack upon him.
Go, unquiet wanderer,
And gather the Glasnevin coverlet
About your head till the dust stops your ear,
The time for you to taste of that salt breath
And listen at the corners has not come;
You had enough of sorrow before death —
Away, away! You are safer in the tomb.

乞丐對著乞丐喊／

「是時候離開這世界了，去某個地方，
在海風中我又找回了我的健康，」
乞丐對著乞丐喊，發了瘋似地喊著，
「在我老死之前去找尋我的靈魂。」

「得到房子和妻子，舒適又甜美，
就得以擺脫我鞋子裡面的惡魔，」
乞丐對著乞丐喊，發了瘋似地喊著，
「還有我雙腿間那個更兇惡的魔鬼。」

Beggar to Beggar Cried

"TIME to put off the world and go somewhere
And find my health again in the sea air,"
Beggar to beggar cried, being frenzy-struck,
"And make my soul before my pate is bare."

"And get a comfortable wife and house
To rid me of the devil in my shoes,"
Beggar to beggar cried, being frcnzy-struck,
"And the worse devil that is between my thighs."

「我還想娶個漂亮的少女，
也不用太漂亮——看得過去就行，」
乞丐對著乞丐喊，發了瘋似地喊著，
「可鏡子裡卻顯現出一個魔鬼。」

「她不必太富有，因為富人
受財產驅使，就像乞丐們瘙癢難忍，」
乞丐對著乞丐喊，發了瘋似地喊著，
「且她不能有詼諧、愉快的語言。」

「然後，在安逸中我將會受到尊敬，
在寧靜花園，靜謐的夜晚傾聽著，」
乞丐對著乞丐喊，發了瘋似地喊著，
「同在巒棧的鵝群中吹起的喧騰。」

"And though I'd marry with a comely lass,
She need not be too comely—let it pass,"
Beggar to beggar cried, being frenzy-struck,
"But there's a devil in a looking-glass."

"Nor should she be too rich, because the rich
Are driven by wealth as beggars by the itch,"
Beggar to beggar cried, being frenzy-struck,
"And cannot have a humorous happy speech."

"And there I'll grow respected at my ease,
And hear amid the garden's nightly peace,"
Beggar to beggar cried, being frenzy-struck,
"The wind-blown clamour of the barnacle-geese."

《演員女王》中的一支歌／

我母親邊逗著我邊唱，
「多麼年輕，你多麼年輕！」
她做了一只金色的搖籃，
掛在柳枝上來回晃動。

「他走了，」我母親唱著，
「當我被扶上了床，」
邊唱著，邊做著針線活兒，
金線銀線來回穿梭。

她扯緊那線咬斷那線，
繡成一件金光燦燦的長袍，
她流淚了，因為她夢想著我
生來本應戴著皇冠。

A Song from The Player Queen

My mother dandled me and sang,

"How young it is, how young!"

And made a golden cradle

That on a willow swung.

"He went away," my mother sang,

"When I was brought to bed,"

And all the while her needle pulled

The gold and silver thread.

She pulled the thread and bit the thread

And made a golden gown,

And wept because she had dreamt that I

Was born to wear a crown.

「當我懷孕時，」我母親唱著，

「我聽到一隻海鷗哭喊，

看到一片黃色的泡沫

濺落在我的大腿上面。」

因此，她怎能不把金色

編織進我的髮辮，

夢想著我應該佩戴

愛情的金冠？

"When she was got," my mother sang,

"I heard a sea-mew cry,

And saw a flake of the yellow foam

That dropped upon my thigh."

How therefore could she help but braid

The gold into my hair,

And dream that I should carry

The golden top of care?

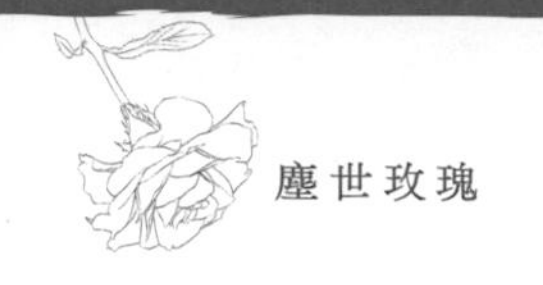

青春的記憶／

那些時光有如在戲中一樣消逝；
我曾擁有過愛情賜予的睿智，
我曾擁有過一份天生的智慧，
儘管我說盡一切，
縱然我得到了她的讚美，
從嚴寒的北方飄來的雲朵，
頓然掩藏了愛的月亮。

我的每一句話都出自真心，
我讚美她的肉體與靈魂，
直到驕傲點亮她的雙眸，
歡樂為她的雙頰抹上紅暈，
虛榮更使她的腳步飄忽起來，
儘管稱頌不已，我們卻
只能找到前面的黑暗。

A Memory of Youth

The moments passed as at a play;

I had the wisdom love brings forth;

I had my share of mother-wit,

And yet for all that I could say,

And though I had her praise for it,

A cloud blown from the cut-throat North

Suddenly hid Love's moon away.

Believing every word I said,

I praised her body and her mind

Till pride had made her eyes grow bright,

And pleasure made her cheeks grow red,

And vanity her footfall light,

Yet we, for all that praise, could find

Nothing but darkness overhead.

我們靜坐著，宛如磐石，

雖然她沒有言語，可我們知道，

即使最完美的愛情也會消亡，

經受無情地摧毀。

要不是愛神聽到

一隻滑稽小鳥的啼叫，

從雲影中拉出絕美的月亮。

We sat as silent as a stone,

We knew, though she'd not said a word,

That even the best of love must die,

And had been savagely undone

Were it not that Love upon the cry

Of a most ridiculous little bird

Tore from the clouds his marvellous moon.

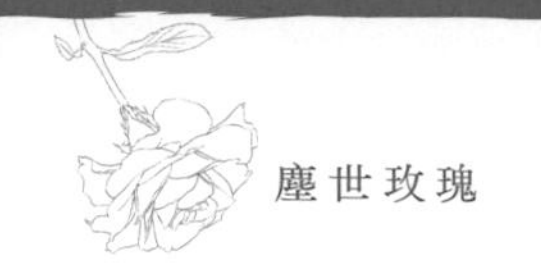

一件外衣／

我把我的歌縫製成一件外衣，

刺滿錦繡，

從古老的神話

擷取構思；

然而愚蠢的人們奪走了它，

在世人的眼前炫耀它，

彷彿是他們親手縫製。

歌啊，就讓他們拿走吧，

因為要有更多進取之心

才敢赤身裸體地行走。

A Coat

I made my song a coat

Covered with embroideries

Out of old mythologies

From heel to throat;

But he fools caught it,

Wore it in the world's eyes

As though they'd wrought it.

Song, let them take it,

For there's more enterprise

In walking naked.

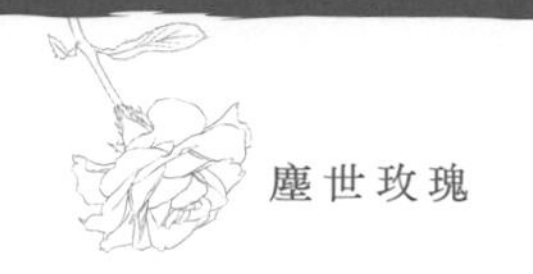

柯爾莊園的野天鵝／

樹木身著美麗秋裝，

林間小徑一片乾枯；

在十月的暮色裡，湖水

映照著靜謐的天空，

而在亂石間蜿蜒的溪水中，

浮游著五十九隻天鵝。

自從我初次計數它們開始，

第十九度秋天已翩然而至，

我還來不及數清，就看到

它們倏地全部飛起；

翺翔在天空，拍著翅膀，發出巨大的聲響，

盤旋成一個大而破碎的圓圈。

The Wild Swans at Coole

The trees are in their autumn beauty,

The woodland paths are dry,

Under the October twilight the water

Mirrors a still sky;

Upon the brimming water among the stones

Are nine-and-fifty swans.

The nineteenth autumn has come upon me

Since I first made my count;

I saw, before I had well finished,

All suddenly mount

And scatter wheeling in great broken rings

Upon their clamorous wings.

我曾凝視過這些光彩奪目的天鵝，

此刻心中卻一片辛酸。

一切都變了，在這湖邊的暮色中，

我初次駐足傾聽，

那頭頂上如鐘鳴般的拍翅聲，

並讓步伐變得輕快。

它們仍不知疲倦，成雙成對，

在清冷的溪水中親密地

滑行或展翅飛入半空；

它們的心依然年輕；

無論漂泊至何方，

它們仍然飽含熱情和征服之心。

此刻，它們正在靜謐的水面上浮游，

神祕而幽雅，

可有一天我醒來，它們早已離去。

哦，它們將在怎樣的水草間棲息築巢，

又將在怎樣的湖岸或池塘令人賞心悅目？

I have looked upon those brilliant creatures,
And now my heart is sore.
All's changed since I, hearing at twilight,
The first time on this shore,
The bell-beat of their wings above my head,
Trod with a lighter tread.

Unwearied still, lover by lover,
They paddle in the cold,
Companionable streams or climb the air;
Their hearts have not grown old;
Passion or conquest, wander where they will,
Attend upon them still.

But now they drift on the still water
Mysterious, beautiful;
Among what rushes will they build,
By what lake's edge or pool
Delight men's eyes, when I awake some day
To find they have flown away?

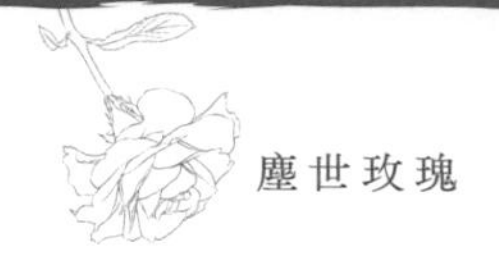

人隨著歲月長進／

我因夢想而憔悴，

像一個風雨剝蝕的石雕海神

屹立在溪流中；

整日裡我都在凝視著

這位女神的美麗，

彷彿我在書中發現的

一幅美人圖畫；

我驚喜於眼睛的充實

或耳朵的聰慧，

欣悅於變得更加智慧，

因為，人隨著歲月長進；

然而，然而，

這是我的夢幻，還是真實？

啊，但願我們曾經相識

當我擁有燃燒的青春之時；

但是我已在夢中慢慢老去，

像一個風雨剝蝕的石雕海神

屹立在溪流中。

Men Improve with the Years

I am worn out with dreams;

A weather-worn, marble triton

Among the streams;

And all day long I look

Upon this lady's beauty

As though I had found in a book

A pictured beauty,

Pleased to have filled the eyes

Or the discerning ears,

Delighted to be but wise,

For men improve with the years;

And yet, and yet

Is this my dream, or the truth?

O would that we had met

When I had my burning youth⊠

But I grow old among dreams,

A weather-worn, marble triton

Among the streams.

致一位少女／

我親愛的，親愛的，我，

比任何人都明瞭，

你為何如此心跳；

即使是在你母親眼中

也沒有我心中雪亮，

誰使我的癡心倍受煎熬，

曾幾何時那狂野的念頭

她卻否認，

或許早已忘掉，

曾使她全身的血液沸騰，

讓眼睛閃耀光芒。

To a Young Girl

MY dear, my dear, I know

More than another

What makes your heart beat so;

Not even your own mother

Can know it as I know,

Who broke my heart for her

When the wild thought,

That she denies

And has forgot,

Set all her blood astir

And glittered in her eyes.

沮喪時寫下的詩行／

何時我最後一次凝視，

它們那綠瑩瑩的眼睛和長長的身軀；

屬於月亮上黑暗中的豹影？

所有狂野的女巫，那些最高貴的婦人，

與她們飛翔的掃把和眼淚，

那憤怒的眼淚，都消失了蹤影。

消失了——那些山巒上神聖的人馬怪獸；

我一無所有，除了那苦悶的太陽，

放逐了，遁去了，那神聖的月亮母親；

如今我已年過半百，

就只能忍受那怯懦的太陽。

Lines Written in Dejection

When have I last looked on

The round green eyes and the long wavering bodies

Of the dark leopards of the moon?

All the wild witches, those most noble ladies,

For all their broom-sticks and their tears,

Their angry tears, are gone.

The holy centaurs of the hills are vanished;

I have nothing but the harsh sun;

Heroic mother moon has vanished,

And now that I have come to fifty years

I must endure the timid sun.

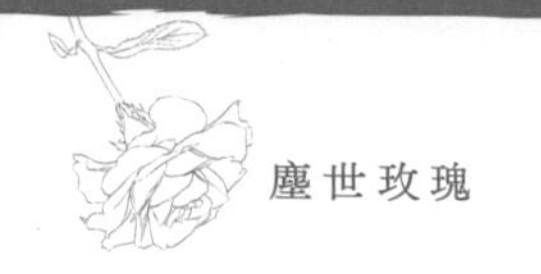

拂曉時分／

那可是我夢的翻版
那位躺在我身邊的女人所夢？
或許我們分享著夢，
當黎明透出第一絲清冷晨暉？

我想：「在本布林本山那邊
有道瀑布，我整個童年時期
都認為無比親切的瀑布；
無論我漫遊足跡有多遠，
我都未曾尋見如此可親的景色。」
我的記憶已把童年所珍視的
美好時光無限地放大與擴展。

Towards Break of Day

Was it the double of my dream

The woman that by me lay

Dreamed, or did we halve a dream

Under the first cold gleam of day?

I thought: "There is a waterfall

Upon Ben Bulben side

That all my childhood counted dear;

Were I to travel far and wide

I could not find a thing so dear."

My memories had magnified

So many times childish delight.

我本想像個孩子一樣地觸摸它，

但知道我的手指只能碰到

冰冷的石頭和水。我發了狂，

甚至興天問罪，因為

它制定的法律中竟有一條是這樣：

我們特別喜愛的東西啊——

都是可望而不可及。

我一直夢著，直到拂曉時分，

鼻息中霧氣冰冷。

但她——躺在我身邊的人，

在更痛苦的夢境中，

望著亞瑟王的那隻神奇的雄鹿，

那隻高大潔白的雄鹿，奔奔跳跳，

從山頂的陡峭走向另一個陡峭。

I would have touched it like a child

But knew my finger could but have touched

Cold stone and water. I grew wild.

Even accusing Heaven because

It had set down among its laws:

Nothing that we love over-much

Is ponderable to our touch.

I dreamed towards break of day,

The cold blown spray in my nostril.

But she that beside me lay

Had watched in bitterer sleep

The marvellous stag of Arthur,

That lofty white stag, leap

From mountain steep to steep.

再次降臨／

轉吧，在向外擴張的旋體上旋轉，

獵鷹再也聽不見主人的呼喚；

一切都四散了；再也保不住中心，

世界上到處瀰漫著一片混亂，

血色的潮水狂奔洶湧，

淹沒了那純真的禮儀；

最優秀的人失去了信念，

最卑鄙的人卻狂熱滿心。

The Second Coming

Turning and turning in the widening gyre

The falcon cannot hear the falconer;

Things fall apart; the centre cannot hold;

Mere anarchy is loosed upon the world,

The blood-dimmed tide is loosed, and everywhere

The ceremony of innocence is drowned;

The best lack all conviction, while the worst

Are full of passionate intensity.

無疑神的啟示就要顯靈，

無疑基督將要再次降臨。

再次降臨！這幾個字還未出口，

出自世界之靈的巨大怪獸

便擾亂了我的視線：荒漠中

人首獅身的形體，

如太陽般漠然無情地相覷，

慢慢挪動雙腿，把荒漠勾勒得一圈又一圈，

沙漠上氣憤的鳥群，翅膀怒拍，陰影飛旋。

黑暗再次降臨，如今我懂得

二十個世紀的沉沉昏睡，

在晃動的搖籃裡闖入惱人的夢魘。

何種野獸，終於等到它的時辰，

懶洋洋地朝向聖地去獲得新生？

Surely some revelation is at hand;

Surely the Second Coming is at hand.

The Second Coming! Hardly are those words out

When a vast image out of Spiritus Mundi

Troubles my sight: somewhere in sands of the desert

A shape with lion body and the head of a man,

A gaze blank and pitiless as the sun,

Is moving its slow thighs, while all about it

Reel shadows of the indignant desert birds.

The darkness drops again; but now I know

That twenty centuries of stony sleep

Were vexed to nightmare by a rocking cradle,

And what rough beast, its hour come round at last,

Slouches towards Bethlehem to be born?

駛向拜占庭／

那並非老年人的國度。

青年人在相互擁抱，還有瀕危的鳥類

在樹林中婉轉放歌。

鮭魚溯遊如瀑布，鯖魚聚集在河面，

飛禽走獸，用整個夏天讚美，

孕育、出生、死亡的一切。

全部沉迷於感性的音樂中，

忽視了不朽的精神祭奠。

老年人不過是無用之物，

拐杖撐起的破衣裳，

除非凡夫俗子的靈魂穿著，

破衣裳拍手唱歌，越唱越嘹亮，

沒有一所歌唱學校不研習

自己輝煌的不朽樂章，

因此我揚帆遠航

駛向神聖的拜占庭。

Sailing to Byzantium

That is no country for old men. The young

In one another's arms, birds in the trees-

Those dying generations-at their song,

The salmon-falls, the mackerel-crowded seas,

Fish, flesh, or fowl, commend all summer long

Whatever is begotten, born, and dies.

Caught in that sensual music all neglect

Monuments of unageing intellcct.

An aged man is but a paltry thing,

A tattered coat upon a stick, unless

Soul clap its hands and sing, and louder sing

For every tatter in its mortal dress,

Nor is there singing school but studying

Monuments of its own magnificence;

And therefore I have sailed the seas and come

To the holy city of Byzantium.

哦，智者們，站在上帝的聖火中，
一如鑲金壁畫中的聖徒，
從聖火中走出來吧，旋轉當空，
來教我靈魂歌唱頌歌，
請燃盡我的心，那執迷於情，
附在垂死肉體的心，將我收留
進入那永恆不朽的絕技裡。

一旦超凡脫俗，我再也不想
用任何自然物構建我的形體；
除非像希臘的金匠鑄造的那樣，
用鍍金或鍛金所鑄造的身影，
使睡意沉沉的君王保持清醒；
或將我放置於一根金枝上歌唱，
唱那過去、現在與未來的事情，
唱給拜占庭的王公和貴婦們聽。

O sages standing in God's holy fire
As in the gold mosaic of a wall,
Come from the holy fire, perne in a gyre,
And be the singing-masters of my soul.
Consume my heart away; sick with desire
And fastened to a dying animal
It knows not what it is; and gather me
Into the artifice of eternity.
Once out of nature I shall never take
My bodily form from any natural thing,
But such a form as Grecian goldsmiths make
Of hammered gold and gold enameling
To keep a drowsy Emperor awake;
Or set upon a golden bough to sing
To lords and ladies of Byzantium
Of what is past, or passing, or to come.

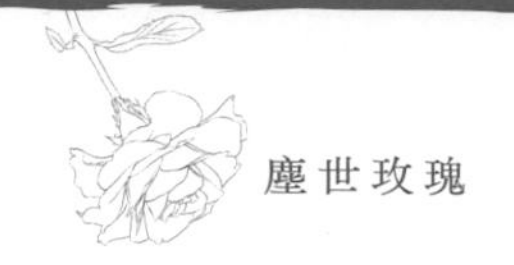

麗達與天鵝／

猛然一擊：碩大的翅膀拍打
在那踉蹌的姑娘頭頂，黑蹼愛撫
她的大腿，硬喙銜著她的脖頸，
把她無助的胸脯緊貼在自己的胸上。
她那受驚的手指又怎能推開——
從鬆開的大腿間推開那光榮的羽毛？
躺在潔白燈芯草叢間的她柔弱身軀
怎能不感覺到那奇特的心跳？
腰股間那一陣顫抖，竟造成
斷壁殘垣，燃燒的屋頂和塔巔，
阿伽門農死去。
就這樣被征服，
這樣被天空中野性的血液所欺凌，
在那一意孤行的喙將她放下之前，
她是否借助他的力量獲得了他的知識？

Leda and the Swan

A sudden blow: the great wings beating still

Above the staggering girl, her thighs caressed

By the dark webs, her nape caught in his bill,

He holds her helpless breast upon his breast.

How can those terrified vague fingers push

The feathered glory from her loosening thighs?

And how can body, laid in that white rush,

But feel the strange heart beating where it lies?

A shudder in the loins engenders there

The broken wall, the burning roof and tower

And Agamemnon dead.

Being so caught up,

So mastered by the brute blood of the air,

Did she put on his knowledge with his power

Before the indifferent beak could let her drop?

在學童中間／

I

我從長長的教室走過，邊走邊詢問著；

戴著白頭巾的和藹的老修女作答解釋；

孩子們學習算術，學習唱歌，

還要學習各種讀物和歷史課本，

學剪裁、學縫紉，樣樣都得乾淨利索，

樣式更要時髦。孩子們的眼睛

時不時帶著好奇的神情，緊緊盯著

一位六十歲含笑的有名人物。

Among School Children

I

I walk through the long schoolroom questioning;

A kind old nun in a white hood replies;

The children learn to cipher and to sing,

To study reading-books and histories,

To cut and sew, be neat in everything

In the best modern way—the children's eyes

In momentary wonder stare upon

A sixty-year-old smiling public man.

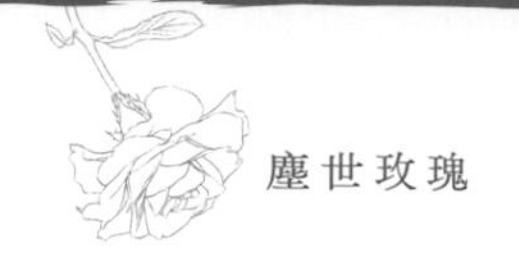

II

我冥想一個麗達那樣的身影，

低俯於一團漸熄的爐火上，講起她的童年

一次粗暴的責備，或瑣碎的事情，

使得童年的一天變成了悲劇——

這一講，仿佛使我們兩顆年輕的心靈

因為同情而交融在一起，

或者，把柏拉圖的比喻略加更改，

化成了蛋殼中的蛋黃和蛋白，渾然一體。

II

I dream of a Ledaean body, bent

Above a sinking fire. a tale that she

Told of a harsh reproof, or trivial event

That changed some childish day to tragedy—

Told, and it seemed that our two natures blent

Into a sphere from youthful sympathy,

Or else, to alter Plato's parable,

Into the yolk and white of the one shell.

III

想起當年那一陣子的悲傷或憤怒，

我看著這裡一個又一個的學童，

想知道當年她是否也有這樣的風度——

因為天鵝的女兒也可能會繼承

涉水飛禽的每一分稟賦——

都會有同樣顏色的秀髮和面容，

這樣一想，我的心怦怦直跳：

她站在我前面，宛如一個活潑的小孩。

IV

她現在的形象飄進了我的腦海中，

這可是十五世紀藝術大師的造詣。

她兩頰深陷，仿佛暢飲著風，

用一堆影子來把自己填飽？

我雖然沒有麗達那樣的品質，

卻也曾有過漂亮的羽衣——夠了，

還不如用微笑回應微笑，來表明

有一種老稻草人日子過得舒舒服服。

III

And thinking of that fit of grief or rage

I look upon one child or t'other there

And wonder if she stood so at that age—

For even daughters of the swan can share

Something of every paddler's heritage—

And had that colour upon cheek or hair,

And thereupon my heart is driven wild:

She stands before me as a living child.

IV

Her present image floats into the mind—

Did Quattrocento finger fashion it

Hollow of cheek as though it drank the wind

And took a mess of shadows for its meat?

And I though never of Ledaean kind

Had pretty plumage once—enough of that,

Better to smile on all that smile, and show

There is a comfortable kind of old scarecrow.

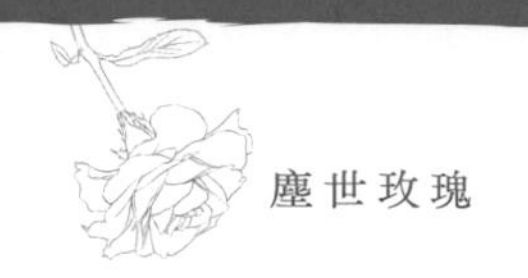

V

一個年輕的母親，膝上緊抱

生殖之蜜所顯露的一個形體，

必須睡呀，叫呀，掙扎著要脫逃，

如記憶或藥物的決定；

倘若她瞥見六十多個冬天來到那個形體的頭上，

她會怎樣看她兒子，

作為對生他時劇痛的一份補償，

或為對他前途擔心的一份補償？

VI

柏拉圖認為自然只不過是泡影，

在幽靈般的事物變幻圖上嬉鬧；

結實的亞裡斯多德揮舞著鞭子，

在一位眾王之王的屁股上面薄施懲戒；

金股骨的畢達哥拉斯，無人不曉，

在一把弓弦上運指彈撥

哪顆星星唱歌和無憂無慮的繆斯們所聽到的歌謠：

舊拐杖披著爛衣衫，去嚇飛鳥。

V

What youthful mother, a shape upon her lap
Honey of generation had betrayed,
And that must sleep, shriek, struggle to escape
As recollection or the drug decide,
Would think her Son, did she but see that shape
With sixty or more winters on its head,
A compensation for the pang of his birth,
Or the uncertainty of his setting forth?

VI

Plato thought nature but a spume that plays
Upon a ghostly paradigm of things;
Solider Aristotle played the taws
Upon the bottom of a king of kings;
World-famous golden-thighed Pythagoras
Fingered upon a fiddle-stick or strings
What a star sang and careless Muses heard:
Old clothes upon old sticks to scare a bird.

VII

修女和母親們都崇拜偶像，

但燭光映照的尊容並不同於

那些激起母親冥思遐想的形象，

而只是使石雕或銅像寧息安生，

但它們也叫人心碎——那存在的情形，

激情、虔誠和慈愛所熟悉的至尊，

還有為所有天國的榮光所象徵的——

哦，對人類事業自生自長的嘲弄者。

VIII

辛勞也就是開花或者舞蹈，

軀體不為取悅靈魂而自殘，

美並非被它自身的絕望所懊惱，

迷糊的智慧也不是出自夜半燈殘。

哦，栗樹啊，根須粗壯繁花興旺，

你是葉子、花朵，還是枝幹？

哦，隨著節拍搖曳的軀體，明亮的眼睛

我們怎樣能辨別舞蹈和跳舞的人？

VII

Both nuns and mothers worship images,

But those the candles light are not as those

That animate a mother's reveries,

But keep a marble or a bronze repose.

And yet they too break hearts—O Presences

That passion, piety or affection knows,

And that all heavenly glory symbolise—

O self-born mockers of man's enterprise;

VIII

Labour is blossoming or dancing where

The body is not bruised to pleasure soul.

Nor beauty born out of its own despair,

Nor blear-eyed wisdom out of midnight oil.

O chestnut-tree, great-rooted blossomer,

Are you the leaf, the blossom or the bole?

O body swayed to music, O brightening glance,

How can we know the dancer from the dance?

路邊的傻子／

當所有的操勞

從搖籃跑向墳墓

又從墳墓跑回搖籃；

而一個傻瓜

纏繞在軸上的思想

也只不過是鬆散的絲線，僅僅是鬆散的絲線。

當搖籃和線軸都已逝去，

我也變成一抹影子。

由某種物質聚成，

像風一樣透明，那時

我想，我會邂逅

一份誠摯的愛情，一份誠摯的愛情。

The Fool by the Roadside

When all works that have

From cradle run to grave

From grave to cradle run instead;

When thoughts that a fool

Has wound upon a spool

Are but loose thread, are but loose thread;

When cradle and spool are past

And I mere shade at last

Coagulate of stuff

Transparent like the wind,

I think that I may find

A faithful love, a faithful love.

夏天和春天／

我們坐在一棵老荊棘樹下，

聊著聊著聊過了一個長夜，

談起我們有生以來

那曾做過的和曾說的一切；

我們講到我們怎樣成人，

獲悉我們曾經分裂了一個靈魂，

如果彼此依偎在對方的懷抱裡，

這樣我們才能融為一體；

這時彼特顯出一副兇狠的表情，

因為，他和她似乎，

就在這棵樹下，一起

訴說過童年的日子。

哦，曾有過怎樣的新芽出綻，

曾有過怎樣的繁花怒放，

當我們享有整個夏天的時候，

她已擁有了整個春天！

Summer and Spring

We sat under an old thorn-tree
And talked away the night,
Told all that had been said or done
Since first we saw the light,
And when we talked of growing up
Knew that we'd halved a soul
And fell the one in t'other's arms
That we might make it whole;
Then Peter had a murdering look,
For it seemed that he and she
Had spoken of their childish days
Under that very tree.
O what a bursting out there was,
And what a blossoming,
When we had all the summer-time
And she had all the spring!

致安妮·葛列格裡／

「絕不會有青年，

因為那披散在你耳旁

蜂蜜色的牆一般的秀髮，

而陷入絕望，

愛你，只是因為你孤單，

不是因為你的金黃頭髮。」

「但我能把頭髮染一染，

把這許多顏色都染上：

棕色，或黑色，或胡蘿蔔色，

那絕望中的年輕人興許

愛我，是因為我孤單，

而並非為了我金黃的頭髮。」

「我聽到一個虔誠的老人

在昨天夜裡宣講，

他找到一段聖經證明，

我親愛的，唯有上帝，

因為你的孤單而愛你，

而不是因為你金黃的頭髮。」

For Anne Gregory

"Never shall a young man,
Thrown into despair
By those great honey-coloured
Ramparts at your ear,
Love you for yourself alone
And not your yellow hair."
"But I can get a hair-dye
And set such colour there,
Brown, or black, or carrot,
That young men in despair
May love me for myself alone
And not my yellow hair."
"I heard an old religious man
But yesternight declare
That he had found a text to prove
That only God, my dear,
Could love you for yourself alone
And not your yellow hair."

選擇／

人的理智被迫做出選擇，

生活的完美，或工作的完美，

如果選擇了後者就必須摒棄

天堂似的宮殿，掙扎於黑暗中。

當故事全部結束，還有何奇聞？

幸運或不幸，勞作已留下了印跡：

舊時的困惑，一隻空癟的錢袋，

或白晝的虛榮，黑夜的痛悔。

The Choice

The intellect of man is forced to choose

Perfection of the life, or of the work,

And if it take the second must refuse

A heavenly mansion, raging in the dark.

When all that story's finished, what's the news?

In luck or out the toil has left its mark:

That old perplexity an empty purse,

Or the day's vanity, the night's remorse.

天青石雕／

我曾聽到歇斯底里的女人們說道，

她們已膩煩調色板和提琴弓，

膩了那永遠樂觀的詩人：

因為每個人都懂，至少也應該懂，

如果不採取激烈的行動，

飛艇和飛機就會出動，

像比利王那樣投擲炸彈，

直到城市被夷為平地。

Lapis Lazuli

I have heard that hysterical women say

They are sick of the palette and fiddle-bow.

Of poets that are always gay,

For everybody knows or else should know

That if nothing drastic is done

Aeroplane and Zeppelin will come out.

Pitch like King Billy bomb-balls in

Until the town lie beaten flat.

大家都在扮演他們的悲劇，

哈姆雷特和李爾王，大搖大擺，

這是奧菲莉亞，那是科德莉亞；

他們，如果最後一幕的時候還在——

那巨大的幕布即將降落——

倘若要無愧於戲中傑出的角色，

就不要中斷他們的臺詞並痛哭。

他們明白哈姆雷特和李爾王的歡樂，

歡樂使一切的恐懼改變了形狀。

所有人都嚮往過、得到過，又失落；

燈光熄了，天國在腦海中閃現——

悲劇達到了它的高潮。

然而哈姆雷特在徘徊，李爾王情緒激動，

最後一幕一下子全都結束，

在成千上萬個舞臺上

不能再增加一寸，重上半磅。

All perform their tragic play,

There struts Hamlet, there is Lear,

That's Ophelia, that Cordelia;

Yet they, should the last scene be there,

The great stage curtain about to drop,

If worthy their prominent part in the play,

Do not break up their lines to weep.

They know that Hamlet and Lear are gay;

Gaiety transfiguring all that dread.

All men have aimed at, found and lost;

Black out; Heaven blazing into the head:

Tragedy wrought to its uttermost.

Though Hamlet rambles and Lear rages,

And all the drop-scenes drop at once

Upon a hundred thousand stages,

It cannot grow by an inch or an ounce.

他們來過，或徒步，或乘船，

或騎馬、驢、騾，或駱駝，

古老的文明已在劍鞘。

他們和他們的智慧再無蹤跡。

不見伽裡瑪科斯的手工藝品，

他曾雕刻著大理石，仿佛那是青銅，

他製出的帷帳，栩栩如生，

當海風吹過，似乎站起，

他塑造的細長長燈罩像一棵棕櫚，

卻只站立了一日。

一切倒塌了又重建，

那些重建的人們充滿了歡愉。

On their own feet they came, or On shipboard,
Camel-back; horse-back, ass-back, mule-back,
Old civilisations put to the sword.
Then they and their wisdom went to rack:
No handiwork of Callimachus,
Who handled marble as if it were bronze,
Made draperies that seemed to rise
When sea-wind swept the corner, stands;
His long lamp-chimney shaped like the stem
Of a slender palm, stood but a day;
All things fall and are built again,
And those that build them again are gay.

雕刻在天青石上的是

兩個中國人，背後還有第三個人，

在他們頭頂飛著一隻長腿鳥，

一種長壽的象徵；

那第三者，無疑是個侍從，

手中捧著一件樂器。

天青石上的每個瑕疵，

每一處無意的裂縫或痕，

好似瀑布或雪崩，

或像那依然積雪的坡峰；

雖然櫻樹或梅樹的枝梢

促使那些中國人爬向

令人神往的半山腰房子，而我

喜歡想像他們坐在那個地方。

那裡，他們凝視著群山、天空，

還有一切悲劇性的景象。

一人要聽悲慟的旋律，

嫺熟的手指開始演奏，

他們皺紋密佈的眼睛啊，他們的眼睛

他們古老的、矍鑠的眼睛，充滿了歡樂。

Two Chinamen, behind them a third,

Are carved in Lapis Lazuli,

Over them flies a long-legged bird,

A symbol of longevity;

The third, doubtless a serving-man,

Carries a musical instrument.

Every discoloration of the stone,

Every accidental crack or dent,

Seems a water-course or an avalanche,

Or lofty slope where it still snows

Though doubtless plum or cherry-branch

Sweetens the little half-way house

Those Chinamen climb towards, and I

Delight to imagine them seated there;

There, on the mountain and the sky,

On all the tragic scene they stare.

One asks for mournful melodies;

Accomplished fingers begin to play.

Their eyes mid many wrinkles, their eyes,

Their ancient, glittering eyes, are gay.

一個瘋狂的少女／

那瘋狂的少女正即興創作她的樂曲、
她的詩篇，在沙灘上翩翩起舞，
她的靈魂早已飛離她的身體，
爬上，跌下，她自己也不知在何處，
躲藏在一只汽船的貨物中，
她跌破了膝蓋，我稱那少女
是一個美麗、高尚的事物，或一度
英勇地失去，又英勇地尋獲的事物。

無論遭遇什麼奇災大難，
她都要承受著絕望的音樂之傷，
傷啊，傷啊，她幻覺凱旋歸來，
在放著行囊之處，
非同尋常的、無可分辨的聲響
唱著：「哦，海洋的饑餓，饑餓的海洋。」

A Crazed Girl

That crazed girl improvising her music.
Her poetry, dancing upon the shore,
Her soul in division from itself
Climbing, falling she knew not where,
Hiding amid the cargo of a steamship,
Her knee-cap broken, that girl I declare
A beautiful lofty thing, or a thing
Heroically lost, heroically found.

No matter what disaster occurred
She stood in desperate music wound,
Wound, wound, and she made in her triumph
Where the bales and the baskets lay
No common intelligible sound
But sang, "O sea-starved, hungry sea."

那些意象／

若是我叫你離開

你那心智的空洞又將何妨？

在風和日麗之中

得到更好的培育。

我從來不曾叫你離開

前往莫斯科或羅馬。

放棄那乏味勞作

把繆斯們請到家。

去尋找那些意象，

那些構成一片荒涼，

構成獅子和處女，

還有娼妓和孩童。

到那半空中尋找

展翅而飛的雄鷹，

認出那五種意象

它們使繆斯歌吟。

Those Images

What if I bade you leave

The cavern of the mind?

There's better exercise

In the sunlight and wind.

I never bade you go

To Moscow or to Rome.

Renounce that drudgery,

Call the Muses home.

Seek those images

That constitute the wild,

The lion and the virgin,

The harlot and the child.

Find in middle air

An eagle on the wing,

Recognise the five

That make the Muses sing.

長腳虻／

但願文明不會沉淪，

偉大的戰役不會落敗，

別讓狗叫，栓好小馬

在遠處的一根柱子上；

我們的主將凱撒在帳裡，

地圖在他面前攤開，

雙眼一片木然，

一手托著額頭。

如長腳虻在河流上飛翔，

他的思維在寂靜中滑動。

Long-legged Fly

That civilisation may not sink,

Its great battle lost,

Quiet the dog, tether the pony

To a distant post;

Our master Caesar is in the tent

Where the maps are spread,

His eyes fixed upon nothing,

A hand under his head.

Like a long-legged fly upon the stream

His mind moves upon silence.

但願高聳入雲的塔被焚燒，

人們追憶起那張臉龐，

如果你要走，腳步放輕

再走進這個寂寥的地方。

一分女人，三分幼童，她以為

沒人注意，便用雙腳

練習從街上學來的吉普賽舞步。

如長腳虻在河流上飛翔，

她的思維在寂靜中滑動。

That the topless towers be burnt

And men recall that face,

Move most gently if move you must

In this lonely place.

She thinks, part woman, three parts a child,

That nobody looks; her feet

Practise a tinker shuffle

Picked up on a street.

Like a long-legged fly upon the stream

Her mind moves upon silence.

但願荳蔻年華的少女

都能找到她們心中的第一個亞當，

關上教皇的教堂大門，

別讓那些小孩進來。

在那邊鷹架上斜躺著的

米開朗基羅。

他的手來回移動，

輕輕地，如老鼠一般。

如長腳虻在河流上飛翔，

他的思維在寂靜中滑動。

That girls at puberty may find

The first Adam in their thought,

Shut the door of the Pope's chapel,

Keep those children out.

There on that scaffolding reclines

Michael Angelo.

With no more sound than the mice make

His hand moves to and fro.

Likc a long-legged fly upon the stream

His mind moves upon silence.

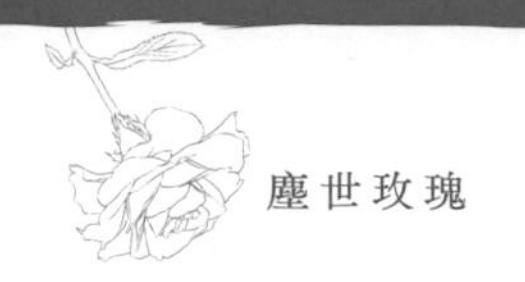

在本布林本山下／

I

請相信在馬理奧提克湖畔的聖徒

所說過的預言，

阿特勒斯的女巫確實知道，

那聖徒的話曾讓群雞啼叫。

請相信那些騎士和美人，

他們超凡脫俗的體態與容貌顯示出他們的神靈，

那臉色蒼白，面容瘦削的同伴，

有著永恆的娟逸，

徹底地贏得了他們的熱情；

此刻他們正在冬日的晨曦裡，

馳騁在本布林本山下。

他們是這麼說的：

Under Ben Bulben

I

Swear by what the Sages spoke
Round the Mareotic Lake
That the Witch of Atlas knew,
Spoke and set the cocks a-crow.
Swear by those horsemen, by those women
Complexion and form prove superhuman,
That pale, long-visaged company
That air an immortality
Completeness of their passions won;
Now they ride the wintry dawn
Where Ben Bulben sets the scene.
Here's the gist of what they mean.

II

人生死輪回多少次，

在兩個永恆之間，

民族的永恆和靈魂的永恆，

古老的愛爾蘭洞悉了這一切；

人無論是壽終正寢，

還是慘遭槍彈的襲擊，

與親人暫時的別離

才是人間最大的恐懼。

雖然掘墓者的勞作艱苦漫長，

然而他們的鐵鍬鋒利，肌肉強壯，

也僅僅是將被埋葬的人

重新捲入人的思緒中。

II

Many times man lives and dies

Between his two eternities,

That of race and that of soul,

And ancient Ireland knew it all.

Whether man die in his bed

Or the rifle knocks him dead,

A brief parting from those dear

Is the worst man has to fear.

Though grave-diggers' toil is long,

Sharp their spades, their muscles strong.

They but thrust their buried men

Back in the human mind again.

III

你曾聽過米切爾的禱告：

「上帝啊，將戰爭降臨在我們這個時代吧！」

你明白，當話說盡，

還有一人正在瘋狂作戰，

淚水從失明已久的眼中滑落，

他將殘缺的心智補全，

片刻之間閒適地駐立，

放聲大笑，心中卻是一片釋然。

甚至那智者在使命實現、

工作認識、夥伴選擇之前，

也會因為某種暴力行為，

心裡總是那麼的惴惴不安。

III

You that Mitchel's prayer have heard,

"Send war in our time, O Lord!"

Know that when all words are said

And a man is fighting mad,

Something drops from eyes long blind,

He completes his partial mind,

For an instant stands at ease,

Laughs aloud, his heart at peace.

Even the wisest man grows tense

With some sort of violence

Before he can accomplish fate,

Know his work or choose his mate.

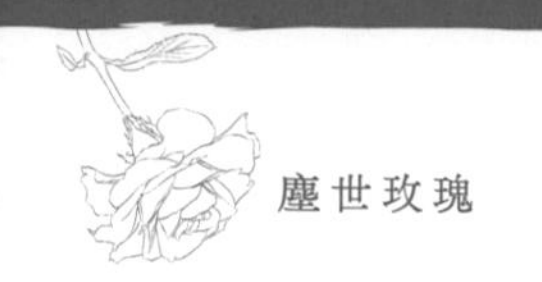

IV

詩人和雕塑家，請盡你們的職責，

莫讓那種時髦的畫家逃離

先人顯赫的豐功偉績，

攜帶靈魂去拜謁上帝，

命他把搖籃適當填滿。

我們開始了力量的衡量：

僵化的埃及人日夜思索形體，

溫雅的斐底亞斯塑造的形狀。

米開朗基羅留下的證據

在西斯廷教堂的屋頂：

只有那半寐半醒的亞當

能撩動周遊世界的貴婦；

心意惶惶，情意激蕩，

證明那工匠祕密的心中

必有其早已確定的目標：

褻瀆人類的至美境界。

IV

Poet and sculptor, do the work,

Nor let the modish painter shirk

What his great forefathers did.

Bring the soul of man to God,

Make him fill the cradles right.

Measurement began our might:

Forms a stark Egyptian thought,

Forms that gentler phidias wrought.

Michael Angelo left a proof

On the Sistine Chapel roof,

Where but half-awakened Adam

Can disturb globe-trotting Madam

Till her bowels are in heat,

Proof that there's a purpose set

Before the secret working mind:

Profane perfection of mankind.

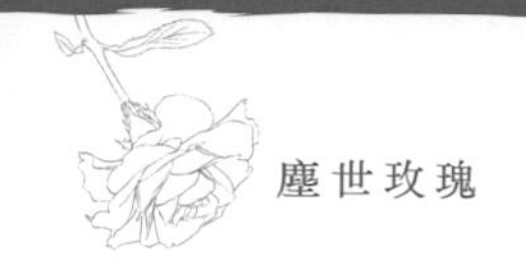

十五世紀義大利的大師，

設計上帝和聖人的背景時，

總是畫著花園，那裡靈魂安詳，

放眼望去——

花朵、芳草，還有無雲的天空，

那些夢幻般的形狀，

彷佛在夢逝去時，只剩下床墊

和床架，依然在聲言

天國的門打開了。

哦，旋轉復旋轉；

一場更大的夢已然消逝，

卡爾弗特和威爾遜、布萊克和克勞德

為信上帝的臣民備好了休息之所，

是帕爾默的話吧，但在那之後

我們的思想就充滿了混亂、憂愁。

Quattrocento put in paint

On backgrounds for a God or Saint

Gardens where a soul's at ease;

Where everything that meets the eye,

Flowers and grass and cloudless sky,

Resemble forms that are or seem

When sleepers wake and yet still dream.

And when it's vanished still declare,

With only bed and bedstead there,

That heavens had opened.

Gyres run on;

When that greater dream had gone

Calvert and Wilson, Blake and Claude,

Prepared a rest for the people of God,

Palmer's phrase, but after that

Confusion fell upon our thought.

V

愛爾蘭詩人，請學好你們的專業，

歌唱那美好創造的一切，

輕視那種面目全非的奧妙，

他們缺乏記憶的頭和心——

低卑的床上的低卑的產品。

歌唱日夜勞作的田間農民，

頌揚策馬疾馳的鄉間紳士，

歌唱修士的虔誠清高

嗜酒後人們猥褻的狂笑；

還要歌唱那些歡樂的王公貴族

在英勇的七個世紀中

屍骨已化成了泥土，

讓你的思緒浸入往昔，

以使我們在將來的時光裡

依然是不屈不撓的愛爾蘭人。

V

Irish poets, earn your trade,

Sing whatever is well made,

Scorn the sort now growing up

All out of shape from toe to top,

Their unremembering hearts and heads

Base-born products of base beds.

Sing the peasantry, and then

Hard-riding country gentlemen,

The holiness of monks, and after

Porter-drinkers' randy laughter;

Sing the lords and ladies gay

That were beaten into the clay

Through seven heroic centuries;

Cast your mind on other days

That we in coming days may be

Still the indomitable Irishry.

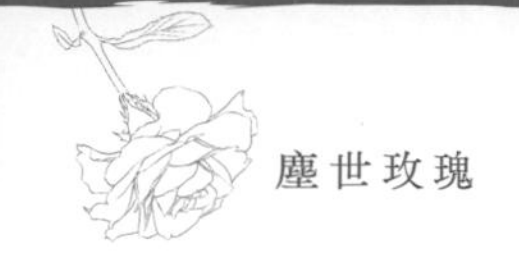

VI

在荒涼的本布林本山下，

葉慈躺在特拉姆克力夫墓地中間。

一個祖先曾是那裡的教區長，

許多年前，一座教堂就在近旁，

在路旁，是一個古老的十字架，

沒有大理石碑，措辭也不同尋常，

在附近採來的石灰石上，

遵他的囑託刻下如下字樣：

對生命，對死亡

投以冷眼

騎士啊，向前！

VI

Under bare Ben Bulben's head

In Drumcliff churchyard Yeats is laid.

An ancestor was rector there

Long years ago, a church stands near,

By the road an ancient cross.

No marble, no conventional phrase;

On limestone quarried near the spot

By his command these words are cut:

Cast a cold eye

On life, on death.

Horseman, pass by!

關於作者

威廉·巴特勒·葉慈（William Butler Yeats，1865—1939），愛爾蘭著名詩人、劇作家和散文家，愛爾蘭文藝復興運動的領袖。

他出生於愛爾蘭一個充滿藝術氣息的家庭，父親拋棄法律改當畫師。小時候的葉慈曾在英國倫敦居住一段時間，因母親時常講述愛爾蘭民間故事，加上與英國同儕的不睦，讓他有了民族意識，在往後時常表現出他對愛爾蘭的赤誠之心。

1884 年葉慈違背父願，丟開油彩、畫布，專心致力於詩歌創作。前期因受莎士比亞、珀西·雪萊影響，詩作大多為浪漫主義風格，以古希臘、印度神話為題材，在 1889 年認識並迷戀愛爾蘭民族主義者茉德·岡後，其詩作更加唯美，將茉德·岡比喻幻化為玫瑰、雅典娜，大量愛情詩就此產生。但隨著茉德·岡的結婚消息，葉慈大受震撼，詩風開始走向抽象、哲學。

民族意識強烈的葉慈，在結識了愛國志士約翰·奧里亞雷後，也開始接觸愛爾蘭本土詩人的作品，作品開始出現愛爾蘭民俗和民間故事。1896 年透過友人牽線認識格雷戈里夫人，與之一同發起愛爾蘭文藝復興運動，日後也合力創立愛爾蘭文學劇院，也就是之後的艾比劇院。

另外，葉慈也對神祕主義和唯靈論有極大興趣。就學時期便曾和朋友創立都柏林祕術兄弟會，之後也曾經擔任黃金黎明協會領袖。在作品《麗達與天鵝》、《塔樓》和《旋梯及其他作品》尤為明顯，其內容皆暗示著歷史運動的軌跡和靈魂輪迴的歷程。

葉慈一生創作豐富，其作品吸收浪漫主義、唯美主義、神祕主義、象徵主義和玄學詩的精華，幾經變革，形成了自己獨特的風格。

1923 年，葉慈獲得諾貝爾文學獎，成為獲此殊榮的第一位詩人。1934 年又獲得哥德堡詩歌獎。晚年葉慈百病纏身，依然筆耕不輟，創作了許多膾炙人口的詩歌，被艾略特譽為「20 世紀最偉大的英語詩人」。

1939 年 1 月 28 日，葉慈最終病逝於法國旅館。

關於作品

葉慈曾於 1923 年獲得諾貝爾文學獎，獲獎的理由是「以其高度藝術化且洋溢著靈感的詩作表達了整個民族的靈魂」。

本書是一部關於愛的詩集，由 80 首詩歌組成，從葉慈 1889 年到 1959 年共 12 部詩集中精選而出。所選詩歌有的節奏低緩，猶如一曲從長巷裡飄出的大提琴曲；有的明亮歡快，宛如愛爾蘭草原上一首優美的風笛曲。

愛貫穿了葉慈的生命，也貫穿於他所有的詩歌當中。在他的人生和詩集裡，愛是嚴肅而又聖潔，美麗而又痛苦的。他將青春、愛情連同死亡一同揉進循環往復、錯綜神祕的時空背景裡互相對視。在這種痛苦的對視中，真理、自由等命題一一浮現，並被賦予了歲月的厚重感。

沒有任何人能夠像葉慈一樣，能將愛情讚頌發展到如此極致，甚至超越愛情中的人而存在。在這久遠、遼闊的時空裡，葉慈在孜孜不倦地構建著自己的、也是人類永恆的命題——生命、尊嚴、青春、愛情，抒寫著他對人類無限的愛。

葉慈生平年表

1865	0	6 月 13 日出生於愛爾蘭的山迪蒙，父親是一名畫家。葉慈家族屬於藝術氣息非常濃厚的家庭，其弟喬治後來成為畫家，兩個姊妹也曾參與工藝美術運動。
1867	2	為了父親約翰·葉慈的畫家事業，全家搬至英國倫敦居住。葉慈與他的兄弟姊妹在家中接受家庭教育，母親蘇珊常常對他們講述愛爾蘭民間故事。
1877	12	葉慈進入葛多芬學校，但成績並不突出。 這時期的葉慈在英國小學受到同儕欺侮，加上前幾年母親所提供的愛爾蘭思想，使他的民族意識更加強烈。
1880	15	因為經濟壓力，葉慈一家遷回都柏林，沒多久移居皓斯。
1881	16	10 月進入伊雷斯摩斯·史密斯中學繼續完成學業，因父親的工作室就在學校附近，葉慈常在此消磨時間，結識許多藝術家及作家。 在這期間，葉慈發現自己喜歡詩歌，開始閱讀莎士比亞等英國作家的作品。
1883	18	開始詩歌創作。初期寫作以古希臘神話作為主要題材，語言風格則受珀西·雪萊影響甚深，較為浪漫唯美。
1884	19	至大都會藝術學校就讀。
1885	20	在《都柏林大學評論》上發表第一部詩作及一篇名《賽繆爾·費格森爵士的詩》的散文。

		一直以來都對唯靈論有濃厚關心，和友人一同創立都柏林祕術兄弟會，並擔任兄弟會領袖。
1886	21	葉慈結識了芬尼亞運動領導人、愛國志士約翰·奧里亞雷。在他的影響下，葉慈開始接觸愛爾蘭本土詩人一些具有民族意識的作品，作品轉向愛爾蘭民俗和民間故事。
1889	24	出版第一本詩集《烏辛之浪跡及其他》。
		認識茉德·岡——一位熱衷於愛爾蘭民族主義運動的女性。她非常仰慕葉慈早年詩作《雕塑的島嶼》，主動和葉慈結識，而葉慈也迷戀上她，劇烈影響了葉慈以後的創作和生活。葉慈曾多次向茉德·岡求婚，卻因二人在民族主義上的意見衝突，均遭到拒絕。
1890	25	葉慈和歐那斯特·萊斯共同創建「詩人會社」，由一群志同道合的詩人們所組成的文學團體，並定期聚會。
1892	27	以茉德·岡為原型創作《凱絲琳女伯爵及其他傳說和抒情詩》，此詩的舞台劇直到 1899 年才得以上演，且後來引發宗教及政治上的諸多爭議。
1896	31	和奧莉薇亞·莎士比亞相戀，一年之後分手。分手後仍維持好友關係，通信 40 餘年。
		透過朋友馬丁認識格雷戈里夫人。這位有著強烈民族思想的女作家鼓勵葉慈投身民族主義運動和戲劇的寫作，給予他理解和支持，她所翻譯的神話故事也為葉慈創作帶來許多靈感。後

		來，葉慈和格雷戈里夫人以及一些其他愛爾蘭作家也共同發起了著名的愛爾蘭文學復興運動。
1897	32	完成詩作《隱密的玫瑰》。
1899	34	葉慈和格雷戈里夫人、馬丁和喬治·摩爾一同創立愛爾蘭文學劇院，希望能讓愛爾蘭文學更加復甦。但這項活動並沒有成功，只維持了兩年，卻促成日後的艾比劇院成立。 詩集《葦間風》問世，獲得當年最佳詩集學院獎，確立了葉慈愛爾蘭詩人的地位，有人認為這部詩集也標誌著現代主義詩歌的開端。
1902	37	資助建立丹·埃默出版社，用以出版文藝復興運動相關的作家作品。這個出版社在 1904 年更名為庫拉出版社。
1903	38	茉德·岡結婚，聽聞此事的葉慈大受打擊，詩風也隨之變化，他拋卻一開始的朦朧美，開始寫較為抽象、哲學的作品。
1904	39	12 月艾比劇院修建。劇院開幕夜上，葉慈的兩部劇作隆重上映。至此之後，葉慈身為劇院董事之一，同時也是劇院的劇作家。
1913	48	認識美國詩人艾茲拉·龐德，龐德對於日本能樂的知識為葉慈提供了靈感，他在 1916 年完成了模仿日本能樂的劇作《鷹之井畔》。
1917	52	九月份，向英國女子喬治·海德李斯求婚，並在當年的 10 月 20 日結婚。
1919	54	2 月 24 日，葉慈的長女安在都柏林出生。
1922	57	被任命為愛爾蘭參議員，任期間推導愛爾蘭貨幣通行及離婚合法化。

1923	58	榮獲諾貝爾文學獎。兩年後發表短詩《瑞典之豐饒》，藉此表達感激之情。
1925	60	晚期，葉慈受神祕主義及印度宗教影響越發顯著，也因此遭受許多抨擊。於是葉慈出版一本嘔心瀝血的散文作品《靈視》，推舉柏拉圖、布列塔諾以及幾位現代哲學家的觀點來證實自己的理論。
1932	67	在都柏林的近郊租了一間房子，安享晚年。這段時間葉慈出版許多詩集、戲劇和散文，包括一生的顛峰之作《駛向拜占庭》，這首詩作體現了葉慈對古老而神祕東方文明的嚮往。
1938	73	出版《威廉．巴特勒．葉慈的自傳》。 這時的葉慈已經體弱多病，於是和妻子前往法國休養。
1939	74	1 月 28 日在法國曼頓的「快樂假日旅館」逝世。最後一首詩作是以亞瑟王傳說為主題的《黑塔》。 逝世後，葉慈起初被埋葬在羅克布呂訥－卡普馬丹，直到 1948 年 9 月才將他的遺體運回愛爾蘭，葬在斯萊戈郡鼓崖的聖科倫巴教堂。

葉慈詩選：塵世玫瑰/威廉.巴特勒.葉慈著；趙靜譯.
-- 初版. -- 臺北市：笛藤出版圖書有限公司,
2022.08
面； 公分
中英對照
譯自：The rose of the world
ISBN 978-957-710-866-1(平裝)
884.151 111012278

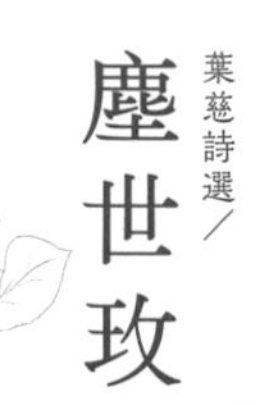

塵世玫瑰 葉慈詩選／ 中‧英對照 雙語版

2022年8月26日 初版第1刷 定價300元

著者	威廉．巴特勒．葉慈
譯者	趙 靜
總編輯	洪季楨
美術編輯	王舒玗
編輯企劃	笛藤出版
發行所	八方出版股份有限公司
發行人	林建仲
地址	台北市中山區長安東路二段171號3樓3室
電話	(02) 2777-3682
傳真	(02) 2777-3672
總經銷	聯合發行股份有限公司
地址	新北市新店區寶橋路235巷6弄6號2樓
電話	(02)2917-8022．(02)2917-8042
製版廠	造極彩色印刷製版股份有限公司
地址	新北市中和區中山路二段380巷7號1樓
電話	(02)2240-0333．(02)2248-3904
郵撥帳戶	八方出版股份有限公司
郵撥帳號	19809050

圖片來源：Unsplash